CLASSICS Illustrated®

Deluxe

#1

THE WIND IN THE WILLOWS

By Kenneth Grahame

Adapted by Michel Plessix

PAPERCUTZ™

New York

The Wind In The Willows
By Kenneth Grahame
Adapted by Michel Plessix
Translation by Joe Johnson
Lettering by Ortho
Jim Salicrup
Editor-in-Chief

ISBN 13: 978-1-59707-096-6 paperback edition
ISBN 10: 1-59707-096-3 paperback edition
ISBN 13: 978-1-59707-095-9 hardcover edition
ISBN 10: 1-59707-095-5 hardcover edition

Printed in China.
Distributed by Macmillan.
10 9 8 7 6 5 4 3 2

Chapter 1

The River Bank_

AS HE DID AT THE BEGINNING OF EVERY SPRING, THE MOLE HAD LAUNCHED INTO A HUGE PROJECT OF CLEANING, DUSTING, POLISHING AND OTHER WORDS ENDING IN "-ING" THAT WERE JUST AS UNPLEASANT. AAAHH AH...

ATCHOO!!

OH BOTHER! HANG SPRING-CLEANING!

THE WHITE-WASHING WILL WAIT TILL TOMORROW!...

OH!

SPRING WAS MOVING IN THE AIR ABOVE. THE CALL OF THE OUTSIDE WAS TOO STRONG...

THE MOLE FELT THE SOFT CARESS OF THE FIRST SUNBEAMS ON HIS FUR. A LIGHT BREEZE WAVED ACROSS THE MEADOW. HE HAD STAYED SECLUDED FOR SO LONG THAT HE'D ALMOST FORGOTTEN ALL THOSE DELIGHTFUL SENSATIONS.

WHILE HE WAS WALKING, HE TOLD HIMSELF THAT IT WAS JOLLY SEEING EVERYONE BUSTLING ABOUT, ESPECIALLY WHEN YOU DIDN'T HAVE ANYTHING ELSE TO DO. THE BEST PART OF A HOLIDAY IS PERHAPS NOT SO MUCH TO BE RESTING YOURSELF, AS TO SEE ALL THE OTHER FELLOWS WORKING.

AS HE WATCHED THE WATER FLOW BY, THE MOLE STARTED DREAMING ABOUT THE STORY OF THIS RIVER, SENT FROM THE HEART OF THE EARTH TO THE INSATIABLE SEA.

HELLO! NICE MORNING ISN'T IT?

I'M THE WATER RAT. AND YOU?

MM...MY PLEASURE. I...I'M THE MOLE.

YES, YES, YES... THE DAY'S GOING TO BE WONDERFUL. HOW NICE IT'LL BE TO TAKE ADVANTAGE OF IT.

HOW ABOUT A PICNIC BESIDE THE RIVER?

OKAY, IT'S DECIDED. GET THE BOAT READY AND I'LL TAKE CARE OF THE LUNCHEON-BASKET.

THERE NOW. ARE YOU READY?

GOODNESS! HOW DID YOU DO THAT?

UHH...I GOT A BIT TANGLED IN THE ROPE, I THINK...

WELL, MY UNFORTU-NATE FRIEND, WE AREN'T ABOUT TO LEAVE YET, HEH?...

THE RAT WAS EXAGGERATING A BIT. LESS THAN AN HOUR LATER, THEY WERE UNDER WAY...

LET'S SEE... I'VE BROUGHT HEADCHEESE, PEPPER SAUSAGE, HAM, PICKLES, A SALAD OF BOILED EGGS - POTATOES, CHIVES, VINAIGRETTE, BRIE, GOAT-CHEESE, A CHILLED ROSÉ, LEMONADE AND STUFF TO MAKE TEA - DO YOU THINK I BROUGHT ENOUGH?

WHAT'S THIS? YOU STILL HAVE A BIT OF ROPE UNDER YOUR COLLAR...

THE MOLE TOLD HIMSELF THAT IT REALLY WAS NICER TO CONVERSE PEACEFULLY ON THE RIVER THAN TO BE SHUT UP AT HOME CLEANING, FOR GOODNESS' SAKE!

THAT'S THE "WILD WOOD," BUT, YOU KNOW, I DON'T GO THERE VERY MUCH...

WHAT LIES OVER THERE?

AREN'T THERE NICE PEOPLE IN THERE?...

OF COURSE, SQUIRRELS AND RABBITS ARE THERE, THEY'RE ALL RIGHT.

WELL... SOME OF THEM. YOU KNOW HOW RABBITS ARE...

THEN THERE'S BADGER. HE ISN'T ALWAYS EASY TO GET ALONG WITH, BUT HE'S A GOOD FRIEND.

HMPH!

AND THEN, THERE ARE WEASELS, FERRETS AND STOATS. THEY'RE ALL RIGHT, TOO, IN A WAY, BUT THEY GET CARRIED AWAY SOMETIMES, AND...

WELL, YOU CAN'T REALLY TRUST THEM... WHAT DO YOU SAY IF WE STOP HERE FOR OUR PICNIC?

8

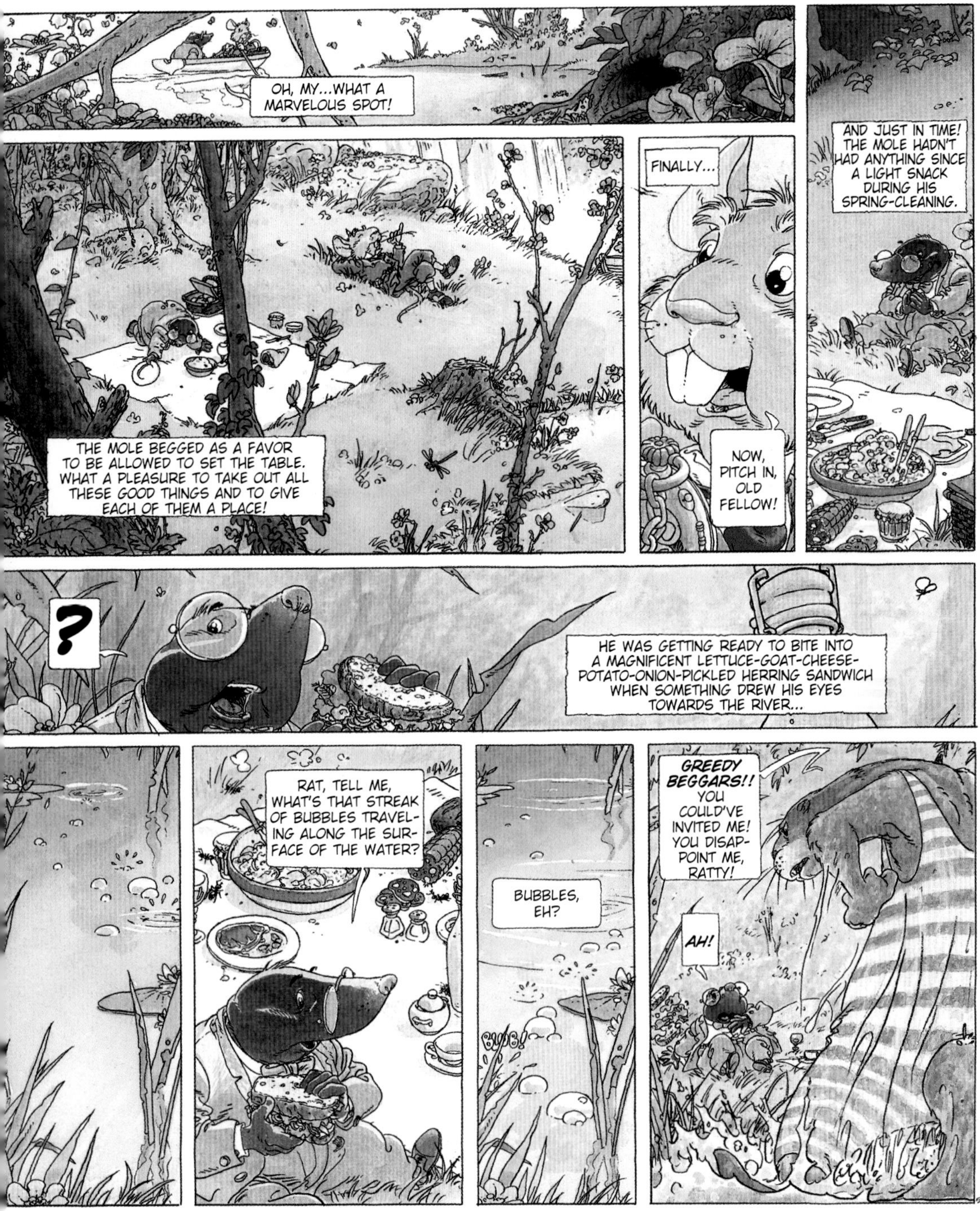

OH, MY...WHAT A MARVELOUS SPOT!
AND JUST IN TIME! THE MOLE HADN'T HAD ANYTHING SINCE A LIGHT SNACK DURING HIS SPRING-CLEANING.
THE MOLE BEGGED AS A FAVOR TO BE ALLOWED TO SET THE TABLE. WHAT A PLEASURE TO TAKE OUT ALL THESE GOOD THINGS AND TO GIVE EACH OF THEM A PLACE!
FINALLY...
NOW, PITCH IN, OLD FELLOW!
?
HE WAS GETTING READY TO BITE INTO A MAGNIFICENT LETTUCE-GOAT-CHEESE-POTATO-ONION-PICKLED HERRING SANDWICH WHEN SOMETHING DREW HIS EYES TOWARDS THE RIVER...
RAT, TELL ME, WHAT'S THAT STREAK OF BUBBLES TRAVELING ALONG THE SURFACE OF THE WATER?
BUBBLES, EH?
GREEDY BEGGARS!! YOU COULD'VE INVITED ME! YOU DISAPPOINT ME, RATTY!
AH!

SORRY, OTTER. THIS WAS AN IMPROMPTU AFFAIR. MY FRIEND MOLE HAD A CRAZY DESIRE TO...BY THE WAY...MR. MOLE.

PLEASED TO MEET YOU. I'M OTTER.

...

WHAT A RUMPUS! THERE'S PEOPLE EVERY- WHERE. I CAME UP THIS BACKWATER TO GET A MOMENT'S PEACE, AND THEN I STUMBLE UPON YOU FELLOWS!

OOPS! EXCUSE ME...THAT'S NOT QUITE WHAT I MEANT, MY FRIENDS...

TWEE TWEE TWEE

CRUNCH

HEY!

WELL, WHAT IS IT NOW?

H'M...' MORNING... H'M...

BADGER! GOOD OLD BADGER! COME JOIN US...

THAT WAS BADGER.

A LITTLE GRUFF, BUT NOT A BAD SORT.

GULF

HAVE YOU SEEN ANY- THING INTER- ESTING ON THE RIVER?

I SAW TOAD. IN A WAGER- BOAT. IT'S NEW.

IN A WAGER- BOAT? TOAD?

HA HA HA HA HA HA HA HA HA HA

WHO'S TOAD?

SPEAK OF THE DEVIL...

LOOK WHO'S COMING ALONG...

TOAD? IT'S... LET'S WATCH AWHILE.

WINE, ANYONE?

THAT'S TOAD FOR YOU.

ONCE, IT WAS NOTHING BUT SAILING...

THEN IT WAS PUNTING. HE SPENT HOURS AND HOURS TRYING TO PUSH HIMSELF WITH HIS POLE.

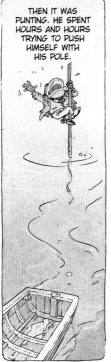

LAST YEAR IT WAS HOUSE-BOATING. WE ALL HAD TO GO STAY WITH HIM THERE AND PRETEND WE LIKED IT. NOW IT'S ROWING...

PLIC!

WHATEVER HE DOES, IT'S ALWAYS THE SAME: HE GETS TIRED AND FINDS A NEW FAD.

HE'S A GOOD FELLOW, BUT NOT STABLE.

PLOUF!

ESPECIALLY IN BOATS...

!

11

EXCUSE ME, PLEASE, GOTTA GO ASSIST TOAD. HE'S IN DANGER...

AND SINCE NO ONE ELSE BUT ME'S GOT A SWIMSUIT...

WELL, WELL, I SUPPOSE WE OUGHT TO BE THINKING ABOUT GOING BACK. I WONDER WHICH OF US WOULD DO BETTER AT CLEARING THE TABLE...

OH, PLEASE... LET ME TRY...

OF COURSE, RAT AGREED. PACKING THE REMAINS OF A PICNIC WAS NOT AS PLEASANT AS UNPACKING IT, BUT THE MOLE HAD DECIDED TO ENJOY EVERYTHING.

POOR MOLE! EACH TIME HE HAD FINISHED FILLING THE BASKET WITH GREAT DIFFICULTY, A FORGOTTEN OBJECT APPEARED. HOW COULD SUCH A SMALL BASKET HAVE HELD SO MANY THINGS?!

AT LAST, THEY COULD DEPART.

ARE YOU SURE YOU DIDN'T FORGET ANYTHING?

NO, NO, YOU CAN TRUST ME.

THE AFTERNOON SUN WAS GETTING LOW. RAT WAS RECITING POEMS TO HIMSELF WHILE DAYDREAMING. AS FOR MOLE, HE WAS VERY FULL OF LUNCH AND OF THE DELIGHTFUL DAY.

"SPRING ALL AROUND
FILLS US ANEW
THIS WORLD OF SOUND
MAKE ME HUNGRY, TOO
THE FROG CROAKS
WHILE THE SPARROW JOKES
I'M READY TO DINE
WITH A FINE GLASS OF WINE."

BURP!

RATTY! PLEASE, I WANT TO ROW, NOW!

NOT YET, MY YOUNG FRIEND. NOT BEFORE A FEW LESSONS. ROWING IS HARDER THAN IT LOOKS. DO YOU REMEMBER TOAD JUST NOW...

BUT I'VE BEEN WATCHING YOU...

OH, NO! ARE YOU CRAZY?!

STOP! YOU'LL HAVE US OVER!

OH...WHAT AN IDIOT I AM! WOULD YOU FORGIVE ME, RAT?

DON'T BE SILLY! WHAT'S A LITTLE WET TO A WATER RAT?

TROT AROUND A LITTLE, TO WARM YOU UP. I'M GOING TO DIVE IN AGAIN TO LOOK FOR THE LUNCHEON-BASKET.

THERE WE GO, THE PROBLEM'S FIXED. COME TO MY HOUSE AND FINISH DRYING OFF TO SOME GOOD HOT WINE.

OH, AND THEN YOU'D DO JUST AS WELL TO STAY FOR AWHILE. IT WOULD DO YOU SOME GOOD...

IN THE FACE OF SUCH KINDNESS, MOLE COULDN'T HOLD BACK AN EMOTIONAL TEAR OR TWO.

RAT KINDLY LOOKED THE OTHER WAY...

BUT NOT US.

THUS, MOLE CAME AND STAYED WITH HIS NEW FRIEND RAT. THE HOT WINE WAS LIGHTLY SCENTED WITH CINNAMON AND LEMON, AND THE GINGERBREAD COOKIES WERE SCRUMPTIOUS.

RAT TOLD STORIES LATE INTO THE NIGHT, STORIES ABOUT FLOODS AND WEIRS, STEAMBOATS AND BOTTLES IN THE WATER, MAGICAL, TERRIBLE STORIES THAT MAKE UP LIFE ALONG THE WATER.

OH YES, TODAY HAD BEEN EXCITING. AND THE FOLLOWING DAYS PROMISED TO BE NO LESS SO.

14

Chapter 11

The Open Road_

"ALL ALONG THE BACKWATER,
THROUGH THE RUSHES TALL,
DUCKS ARE A-DABBLING,
UP TAILS ALL!
DUCKS' TAILS, DRAKES' TAILS,
YELLOW FEET A-QUIVER..."

DID YOU COMPOSE THAT SONG? THE DUCKS MUST NOT BE VERY FOND OF IT...

NO, NOT REALLY.

THEY SAY THAT THEY DO WHAT THEY WANT WHEN THEY WANT AND HOW THEY WANT. AND IT'S NOT FOLKS SITTING ON THE BANKS WATCHING THEM AND DOING NOTHING WHO HAVE ANYTHING AT ALL TO SAY ABOUT IT...

WON'T YOU TAKE ME TO CALL ON MR. TOAD? I'VE HEARD SO MUCH ABOUT HIM...SHALL WE?

GOOD OLD TOAD, BARON TADPOLE...WHAT A TIMELY IDEA, MOLE! LET'S GET OUT THE BOAT.

IDLERS! SCOUNDRELS!

TELL ME A LITTLE ABOUT TOAD.

HE'S A GOOD FRIEND. OF COURSE, HE ISN'T VERY CLEVER, BUT RATHER BOASTFUL AND EASILY FRIGHTENED, TESTY AND NAIVE, PROUD AND A LITTLE COWARDLY. BUT HE HAS HIS QUALITIES.

OH, I SEE.

AH, HERE WE ARE...

AND HERE IS THE MODEST RESIDENCE OF LORD BARON TADPOLE: "TOAD HALL."

REALLY? THAT LITTLE WHITE CABIN THERE UNDER THE WILLOW?

IT LOOKS LIKE TOAD HAS TIRED OF BOATING.

AH, THERE HE IS.

HMM, HE SEEMS TO BE DAYDREAMING TO ME.

MY FRIENDS! MY GOOD FRIENDS!

WHAT A SPLENDID SURPRISE! I WAS JUST GOING TO SEND SOMEONE TO LOOK FOR YOU!

DO YOU WANT SOMETHING TO DRINK?

ICED TEA? CURRANT JUICE?

PLEASE, HAVE A SEAT...

IT'S VERY PRETTY HERE.

PRETTY? THANK YOU. I CAN ASSURE YOU THAT THIS IS THE FINEST HOUSE ON THE WHOLE RIVER.

OR ANYWHERE ELSE!

PUFF PUFF

WINK

?

WINK

ALL RIGHT, YOU GOT ME...YOU KNOW WHAT A BRAGGART I CAN BE, RATTY. YOU CAN'T CHANGE ME.

BUT THEN...YOU DON'T HAVE SUCH A BAD TIME IN THIS HOUSE IT SEEMS TO ME.

SO THERE. I WANTED TO TALK TO YOU ABOUT A PROJECT. A GREAT PROJECT...NOTHING TO DO WITH THAT SILLY BOATING!

13.

17

COME WITH ME TO THE STABLE-YARD, YOU'LL UNDERSTAND BETTER.

TSK! TSK!

SLURP!!

HERE'S THE LIFE FOR YOU, GENTLEMEN, THE GENUINE OCCUPATION FOR A LIFE-TIME. TRAVELING, LETTING YOURSELF GO AT THE WHIM OF THE PATHS, WEARING SHOES OF WIND...

WAKING UP EVERY MORNING TO A NEW SCENE, EATING IN NEW INNS EVERY NIGHT, GOING FROM VERDANT FORESTS TO LOST CITIES, JOURNEYING THROUGH BEAUTIFUL AND DANGEROUS UNKNOWN COUNTRIES LETTING YOURSELF BE CARRIED ALONG ON THE BACKBONE OF THE WORLD...

DO YOU SEE JUST HOW FINE MY "WHEELBAR-ROW" IS? I DID IT ALL MYSELF! I EVEN CHOSE THE DECORATOR!

COME IN, ADMIRE THE CRAFT WORK...

HMM... VERY NICE TASTE...

MOLE APPRECIATED THE SOFTNESS OF THE EMBROI-DERED CUSHIONS WHILE TOAD DEMONSTRATED ALL SORTS OF LITTLE CONTRAPTIONS.

AS YOU CAN SEE, EVERY-THING IS READY FOR OUR DEPARTURE THIS AFTERNOON.

EXCUSE ME, TOAD...

DID YOU SAY "OUR" DEPAR-TURE?

OF COURSE! WHY DO YOU THINK I HAD YOU COME? I SIMPLY CAN'T MANAGE WITHOUT YOU! THIS EXPERIENCE WILL MAKE NEW ANIMALS OUT OF YOU, REAL ONES!

YOU'RE SURELY NOT GOING TO SPEND YOUR WHOLE LIFE IN YOUR BOAT ARE YOU?!

BUT I LOVE BOATING! I LOVE MY LIFE ON THE RIVERBANK!

AND MOLE TOO! DON'T YOU, MY FRIEND?

WELL... YES, OF COURSE, UH...

...NOT EVEN A WEE LITTLE SPIN?

18

RAT WASN'T VERY EXCITED ABOUT THE PROSPECTS OF THIS TRIP. BUT WITH THE HELP OF THE WINE, AND BECAUSE OF THE COMPLACENT ENTHUSIASM OF MOLE, HE ENDED UP GIVING IN TO TOAD'S DELIRIOUS PROJECT.

YES, YES, YES, THAT'S IT, A LITTLE NOTHING SPIN, AND AFTER- WARDS WE'LL SEE...COME ON, WE'LL TALK ABOUT IT OVER A GOOD MEAL.

IT WAS STILL NECESSARY TO CONVINCE THE OLD HORSE WHO PREFERRED THE SECURITY OF HIS PADDOCK TO WHO KNOWS WHAT ADVENTURE, AND THEN TO GATHER SEVERAL INDISPENSABLE ITEMS THAT TOAD HAD FORGOTTEN.

AT LAST, IT WAS TIME TO DEPART...

THE BIRDS IN THE ORCHARDS, AS WELL AS ALL THAT RAN, JUMPED, CLIMBED AND CRAWLED, SEEMED TO GREET THEM AS THEY PASSED. THE AIR WAS DELICATELY SCENTED WITH HUMID WOOD AND THE INTERMITTENT DRONING OF THE FLYING BUGS ACCOMPANIED THEM.

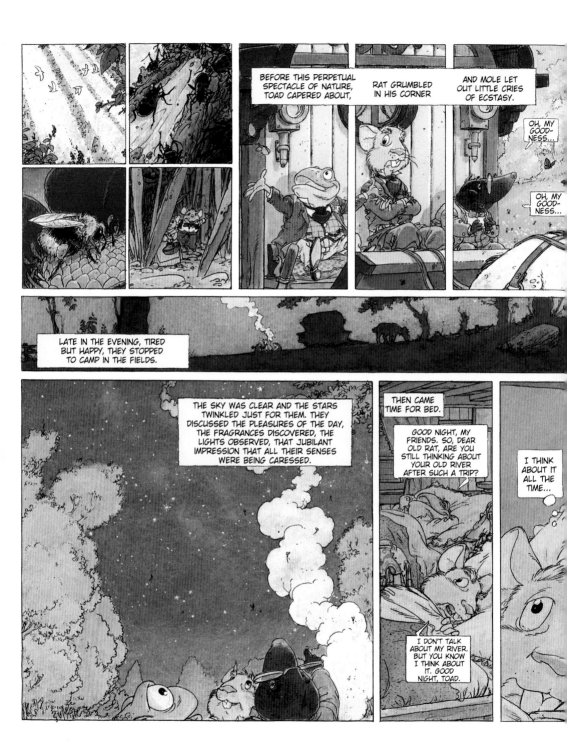

BEFORE THIS PERPETUAL SPECTACLE OF NATURE, TOAD CAPERED ABOUT,

RAT GRUMBLED IN HIS CORNER

AND MOLE LET OUT LITTLE CRIES OF ECSTASY.

OH, MY GOODNESS...

OH, MY GOODNESS...

LATE IN THE EVENING, TIRED BUT HAPPY, THEY STOPPED TO CAMP IN THE FIELDS.

THE SKY WAS CLEAR AND THE STARS TWINKLED JUST FOR THEM. THEY DISCUSSED THE PLEASURES OF THE DAY, THE FRAGRANCES DISCOVERED, THE LIGHTS OBSERVED, THAT JUBILANT IMPRESSION THAT ALL THEIR SENSES WERE BEING CARESSED.

THEN CAME TIME FOR BED.

GOOD NIGHT, MY FRIENDS. SO, DEAR OLD RAT, ARE YOU STILL THINKING ABOUT YOUR OLD RIVER AFTER SUCH A TRIP?

I THINK ABOUT IT ALL THE TIME...

I DON'T TALK ABOUT MY RIVER. BUT YOU KNOW I THINK ABOUT IT. GOOD NIGHT, TOAD.

RAT, TOMORROW, IF YOU WANT, I'LL GO WITH YOU TO THE RIVER.

THANK YOU, MOLE, BUT I CAN'T LEAVE TOAD ALL ALONE, DOING STUPID STUFF. IT WON'T TAKE VERY LONG...

TOAD'S FADS NEVER DO. IT'LL BE OVER SOON...

HE DIDN'T KNOW HOW RIGHT HE WAS...

TOAD, HEY TOAD...IT'S ALREADY BROAD DAYLIGHT.

ET IT GO, OLD MAN. YOU'RE WASTING YOUR TIME.

BECAUSE THEY HAD NO CHOICE, OUR TWO FRIENDS DIVIDED THE CHORES BETWEEN THEM: CARING FOR THE OLD HORSE, GATHERING WOOD AND LIGHTING THE FIRE...

...GOING TO BUY A BUNCH OF THINGS THAT TOAD HAD FORGOTTEN TO PROVIDE, WASHING THE PREVIOUS EVENING'S DISHES...

...MAKING BREAKFAST...

WHEW...LET'S TAKE A BREAK WHILE THE TEA STEEPS...

AAAH, MY FRIENDS, SEE HOW PLEASANT AND EASY LIFE IS COMPARED TO THE ANNOYANCES OF KEEPING HOUSE!

WELL, NOW? WHY ARE YOU LOOKING AT ME LIKE THAT? WHAT DID I SAY?

THAT DAY, THEY DISCOVERED A DELIGHTFUL LITTLE LANE THAT CROSSED THE GRASSY DOWNS. THE GORSE WAS GOLDEN AND THE STORMY WEATHER ADDED VERY BEAUTIFUL LIGHT AND COLORS TO THE PICTURE.

MOLE WAS IN HEAVEN. HE HAD TAKEN OUT HIS LITTLE NOTEBOOK AND TRIED TO GET DOWN EVERYTHING HE SAW.

DID I TELL YOU THAT MOLE HAD LITTLE PADS IN WHICH HE DREW ALL THAT HE HAD EXPERIENCED DURING THE DAY?

HERE, IT'S TOAD WHO SPONTANEOUSLY AND WITH GREAT ENTHUSIASM AGREES TO PARTICIPATE IN THE DAILY CHORES...

THERE, IT'S TOAD CLAIMING HE'S ACHING SO HE CAN BE SERVED BREAKFAST IN BED...

THERE, IT'S TOAD GETTING UP...

AND THERE FINALLY, IT'S OUR FRIENDS WHO'VE GOTTEN UNDER WAY AGAIN.

MOLE WAS TALKING WITH THE OLD HORSE WHO HAD COMPLAINED THAT HE WAS BEING FRIGHTFULLY LEFT OUT OF IT TILL NOW - THE PROOF BEING THAT NO ONE HAD EVEN ASKED HIM HIS NAME. TOAD WAS CARRYING ON A MONOLOGUE AND RAT WAS DREAMING ABOUT HIS RIVER...

WHEN DESTINY CAME ON THE SCENE.

22

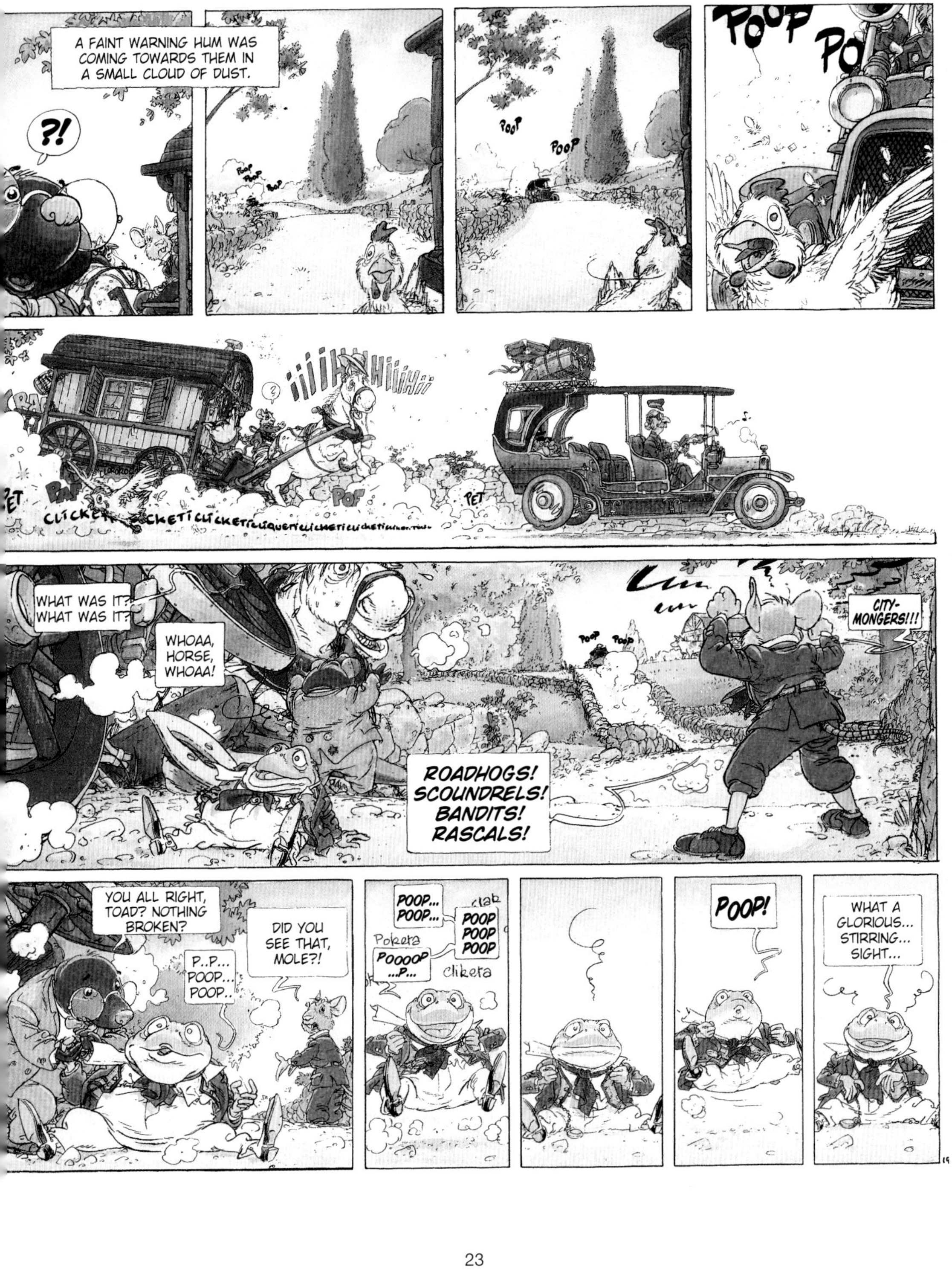
A FAINT WARNING HUM WAS COMING TOWARDS THEM IN A SMALL CLOUD OF DUST.
?!
POOP
POOP
POOP POOP
PAF
POF
PET
WHAT WAS IT? WHAT WAS IT?
WHOAA, HORSE, WHOAA!
CITY-MONGERS!!!
ROADHOGS! SCOUNDRELS! BANDITS! RASCALS!
YOU ALL RIGHT, TOAD? NOTHING BROKEN?
P..P... POOP... POOP..
DID YOU SEE THAT, MOLE?!
POOP... POOP...
POOP POOP POOP
POOOOP ...P...
POOP!
WHAT A GLORIOUS... STIRRING... SIGHT...

WHAT'S WRONG WITH HIM?

IT WAS TOO LATE...TOAD HAD BLOWN HIS FUSES, SHORT-CIRCUITED HIS TIMER, OVERLOADED THE CIRCUIT-BREAKER. IN SHORT, HE'D LOST HIS HEAD.

THE AUTOMOBILE, THE SMELL OF TAR AND EXHAUST FUMES HAD BECOME TOAD'S NEW IDOLS.

THERE WAS NOTHING TO BE DONE. EXCEPT WAIT FOR THIS NEWEST FOLLY TO PASS. LIKE THE OTHERS.

ALL THE SAME, THIS CRISIS SEEMED WORSE THAN USUAL.

THE ONLY THING RAT AND MOLE COULD DO WAS TO LEAD THE STILL HYPNOTIZED TOAD TOWARDS THE NEAREST TRAIN STATION.

THE OLD HORSE WOULD RETURN ON FOOT. HE KNEW THE WAY.

A FEW WEEKS LATER, AT THE RIVER-BANK, OUR TWO FRIENDS LEARNED THAT TOAD HAD ORDERED A MOTOR-CAR IN TOWN.

THERE WOULD SOON BE PROBLEMS.

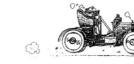

24

Chapter III

The Wild Wood_

THE MOLE HAD LONG WANTED TO MAKE THE ACQUAINTANCE OF BADGER.

BUT EACH TIME MOLE BROUGHT IT UP, RAT PUT HIM OFF.

VISIT HIM? DON'T DREAM OF IT! HE DETESTS BEING BOTHERED.

BESIDES, WE'D HAVE TO CROSS THE WILD WOOD, AND I DON'T THINK THAT'S A GOOD IDEA FOR THE MOMENT...

YES, YES, MOLE...WE'LL SEE ABOUT IT ONE DAY...

NO, WE CAN'T INVITE HIM...HE HATES RECEPTIONS AND FASHIONABLE GATHERINGS.

IT WAS NEVER THE MOMENT! WHICH ONLY SERVED TO AROUSE MOLE'S CURIOSITY ALL THE MORE...

 AND TIME DIDN'T BLUNT THIS CURIOSITY. QUITE THE CONTRARY.

 MUCH WATER HAD FLOWED IN THE SHADOWS OF THE WILLOWS SINCE RAT AND MOLE HAD MET, CARRYING THE DAYS AND SEASONS AWAY WITH IT.

 THE SEASONS... MOLE RECOLLECTED...

 SUCH MAGNIFICENT ILLUSTRATIONS HAD BEEN OFFERED TO THEM! WHAT THEY'D SEEN WAS WORTH ALL THE WORLD'S MUSEUMS...

 AND IT WASN'T OVER! EXCEPT THAT WALKS GREW LESS FREQUENT DUE TO THE WEATHER.

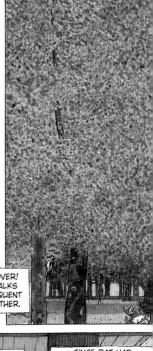

 SO MOLE REMEMBERED AND TRIED TO SET MEMORIES DOWN IN HIS LITTLE PADS.

AND BADGER? HOW WAS HE SPENDING THE LAST DAYS OF AUTUMN?

 BADGER!

SINCE RAT HAD DROPPED OFF TO SLEEP, MOLE DECIDED TO TAKE THE OPPORTUNITY TO GO VISIT HIM!

IT WAS A FINE, AUTUMN AFTERNOON. A DRY COLD BRUSHED MOLE'S PLUMP CHEEKS.

HE HAD NEVER SEEN THE COUNTRY LIKE THIS...

HE FELT LIKE HE WAS DISCOVERING THE BARE BONES OF THINGS...

THE DELLS, THE COPSES, SO SECRETIVE HERETOFORE, NOW EXPOSED THEIR MOST HIDDEN INTIMACIES TO HIM...

NO MORE GARLANDS OF VINES NOR THE FINERY OF FLOWERS AND LEAVES...

NATURE OFFERED HERSELF TO HIM. NUDE. POOR. REAL.

WITHOUT EVER REALIZING IT, MOLE HAD ENTERED THE WILD WOOD...

AT FIRST GLANCE, THERE WAS NOTHING REALLY TO ALARM HIM. DEEP DOWN, RAT REALLY WAS A SCAREDY-CAT.

MOLE EVEN FOUND THESE WOODS RATHER PRETTY.

AN ODOR OF HUMUS AND MUSHROOMS FILLED HIS NOSTRILS...

THE TWISTED ROOTS AND BRANCHES RESEMBLED VAGUELY FAMILIAR FORMS...

PFFF.. HA HA

ESPECIALLY SOME OF THEM.

THEN THE PATTERING BEGAN.

28

THEN NOTHING.

THEN THE FACES BEGAN.

YET MOLE COULD HAVE SWORN HE'D SEEN TWO SMALL, PIERCING EYES A SECOND BEFORE...

HE STARTED OFF AGAIN, TRYING TO CONCEAL AS MUCH AS POSSIBLE HIS GROWING WORRY.

THERE! THOSE EYES AGAIN!

... AND THERE!

AND THERE, TOO!

HOLES EVERYWHERE. EYES EVERYWHERE. HARD-EYED AND HATEFUL. EVIL AND DIABOLICAL. MOLE FELT HIS HAIR STANDING ON END.

THEN THE WHISTLING BEGAN.

oAAAHHH... I THINK I DOZED OFF A BIT...

WHAT DO YOU SAY ABOUT THIS, MOLY?

"THE HERON WITH THE LONG BEAK FITTED WITH A LONG NECK HAD NOTHING DRY ON UP TO HIS KNEES"

SO, MOLY? DOES THAT LEAVE YOU SPEECHLESS?

MOLE?

I KNEW IT!!

HIS SCARF'S GONE. HE MUST HAVE WANTED TO VISIT BADGER.

AND TO DO THAT, HE MUST CROSS THE WILD WOOD.

CRAZY MOLE!

THE WILD WOOD...POOR MOLE!

POOR MOLE...

THE PATTERINGS... THE RUSTLINGS...EVER NEARER...

MORE AND MORE OF THEM!

GET OUT. GET OUT OF HERE. GET OUT OF THIS CURSED PLACE. RUN AWAY. FLEE. *AFRAID.*

CRUNCH

AHHH!

HIDE, YOU FOOL!

OHH, IT WAS ONLY A RABBIT...

HIDE...YES OF COURSE, BUT WHERE?

OH!

30

SAFE?

BY NOW, RAT HAD ALSO ENTERED THE WILD WOOD.

OK.

"IT'S ME THE FEARSOME RATTY! ♪ I THRASH A BULLY BATTY, I BUST HIM IN THE CHOPS I PULL OUT ALL THE STOPS I SNATCH HIS HAIR TWIST HIS NOSE THERE I'M THE PITILESS RATTY!..."

AND MOLE?

FOR THE MOMENT, HIDING IN THE BASE OF THE TREE, HE SEEMED OUT OF DANGER. FOR HOW LONG?

Crrrrk

?!

SUDDENLY A BRANCH CRACKS. THERE. OUTSIDE.

Crrrk

IT WAS GETTING CLOSER...WHAT COULD IT BE?...

AH!

27

31

HEY, MOLY, IT'S ME...

RAT! RATTY! MY GOOD FRIEND! IF ONLY YOU KNEW!

OKAY, IT'S ALL OVER.

I...I JUST WANTED TO VISIT BADGER ,...SNIFF.

SILLY FOOL, I TOLD YOU IT WASN'T A GOOD IDEA.

OH, RAT, PLEASE, DON'T SCOLD ME... I'VE BEEN PUN-ISHED ENOUGH AS IT IS... I'M AFRAID AND I'M COLD...

AND I'M TIRED...

OKAY. LET'S WAIT FOR IT TO SETTLE DOWN OUT THERE. REST AWHILE, I'LL KEEP GUARD.

PEOPLE SAY THAT THE RAT IS A GOOD FRIEND, THAT HE NEVER LEAVES A FRIEND ON HIS OWN. NO DOUBT THAT'S WHY HE WAS-N'T LONG IN REJOINING THE MOLE IN THE KINGDOM OF MORPHEUS...

SEVERAL HOURS PASSED THUS, AS THOUGH BETWEEN PARENTHESES.

Zooo!

SNORE!

Clic!

HULLO! HULLO! HERE - IS - A - GO!...HEY, MOLE! WAKE UP!

32

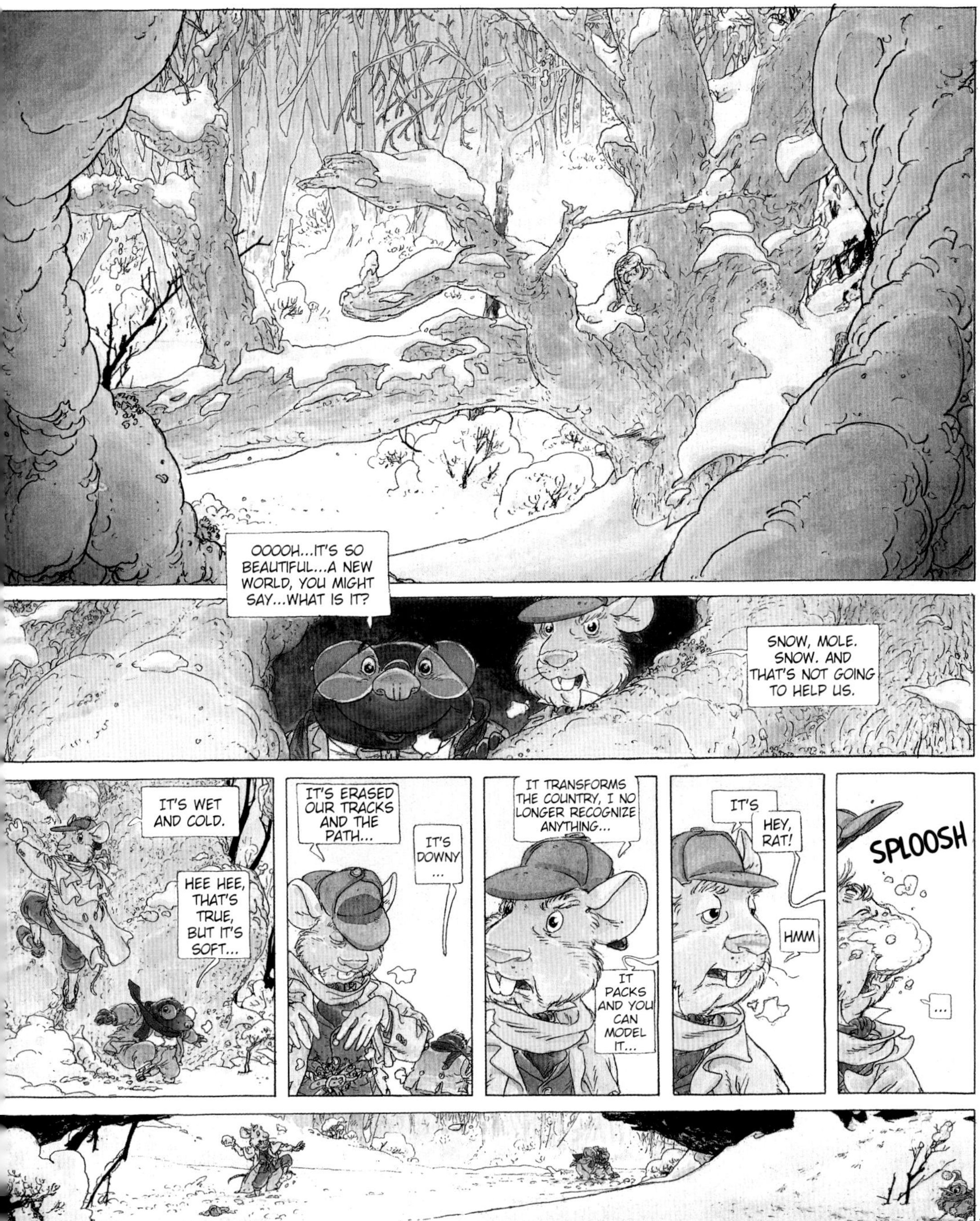
OOOOH...IT'S SO BEAUTIFUL...A NEW WORLD, YOU MIGHT SAY...WHAT IS IT?
SNOW, MOLE. SNOW. AND THAT'S NOT GOING TO HELP US.
IT'S WET AND COLD.
HEE HEE, THAT'S TRUE, BUT IT'S SOFT...
IT'S ERASED OUR TRACKS AND THE PATH...
IT'S DOWNY ...
IT TRANSFORMS THE COUNTRY, I NO LONGER RECOGNIZE ANYTHING...
IT PACKS AND YOU CAN MODEL IT...
IT'S
HEY, RAT!
HMM
SPLOOSH
...
29.

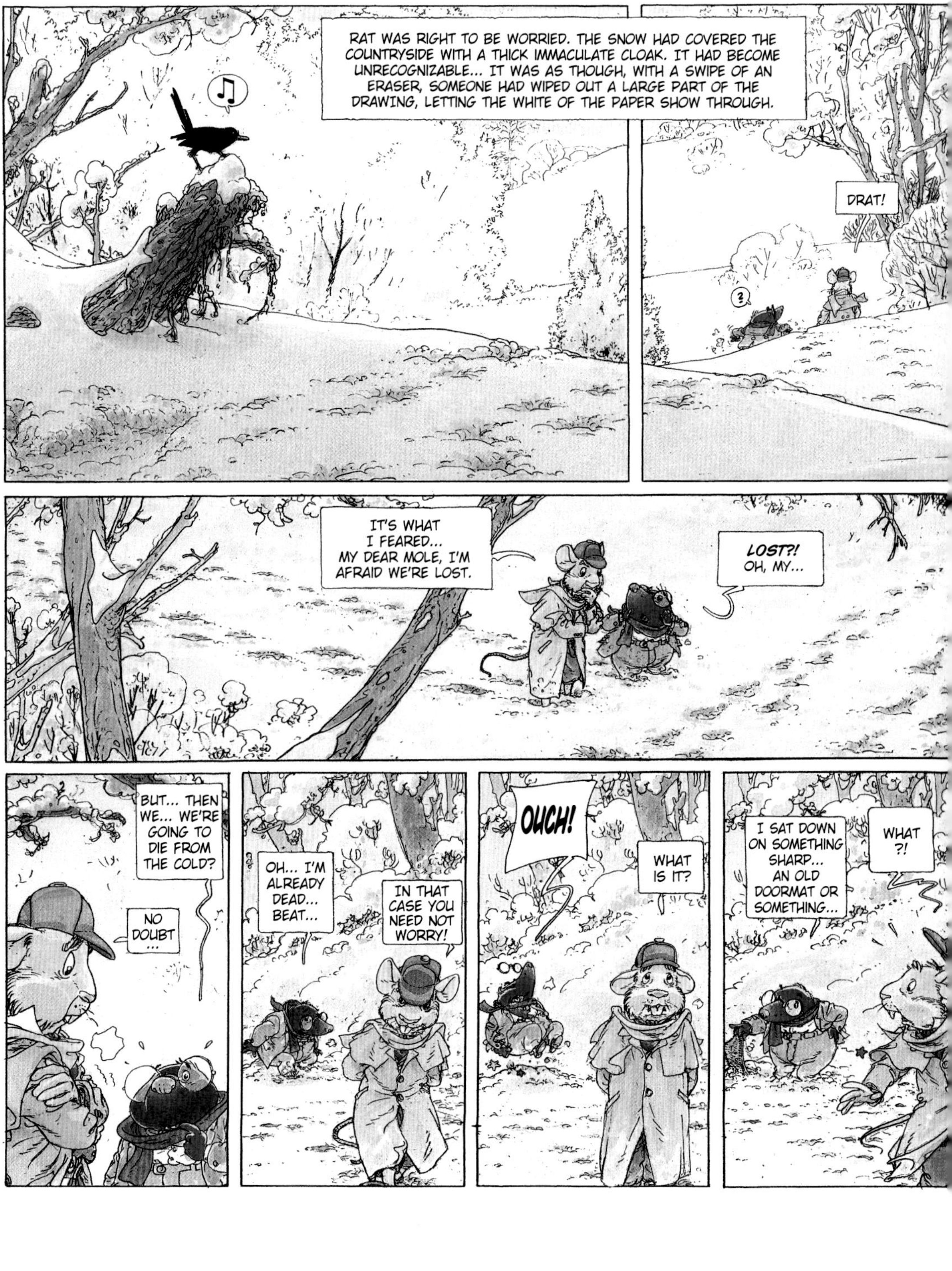
RAT WAS RIGHT TO BE WORRIED. THE SNOW HAD COVERED THE COUNTRYSIDE WITH A THICK IMMACULATE CLOAK. IT HAD BECOME UNRECOGNIZABLE... IT WAS AS THOUGH, WITH A SWIPE OF AN ERASER, SOMEONE HAD WIPED OUT A LARGE PART OF THE DRAWING, LETTING THE WHITE OF THE PAPER SHOW THROUGH.
DRAT!
?
IT'S WHAT I FEARED... MY DEAR MOLE, I'M AFRAID WE'RE LOST.
LOST?! OH, MY...
BUT... THEN WE... WE'RE GOING TO DIE FROM THE COLD?
NO DOUBT ...
OH... I'M ALREADY DEAD... BEAT...
IN THAT CASE YOU NEED NOT WORRY!
OUCH!
WHAT IS IT?
I SAT DOWN ON SOMETHING SHARP... AN OLD DOORMAT OR SOMETHING...
WHAT ?!

♪ HE'S FOUND A DOOR-MAT, HOO-RAY, RA-TA-TAT, HE'S FOUND A DOORMAT, LET'S DIG, DIG, DIG AT THAT. ♪

COME ON, RAT, HAVE YOU LOST YOUR MIND TO BE DANCING ABOUT WHEN SOME UNFORTUNATE SOUL HAS MISLAID HIS DOOR-SCRAPER?

THE POOR THING, HE'S GOING TO BE UPSET NOW...

I HAVE AN IDEA! WE'LL BRING IT BACK TO HIM!

YES, BUT HOW CAN WE FIND HIM.

MOLE! COME LOOK...

OH! BADGER'S HOUSE!! RAT, YOU'RE A REAL DETECTIVE!

ELEMENTARY, MY DEAR MOLE. IF YOU SAY DOOR-MAT, YOU'RE SAYING DOORWAY! AND AROUND HERE, WHO OTHER THAN BADGER WOULD HAVE A DOOR WITH A DOORMAT?

THE FERRETS, WEASELS AND OTHER STOATS AREN'T THE KIND TO TEND TO SUCH THINGS...

SO... ARE WE SAFE?

YES, IF BADGER'S HOME...

KNOCK KNOCK

♪ DINGAYNG, DINGAYNG

AND WHILE OUR FRIENDS DUELED AWAY, ONE ON THE DOOR, ONE ON THE BELL, MOLE THOUGHT HE HEARD THE FEEBLE SOUND OF A STEP COMING TO HIM FROM DEEP IN THE GROUND. BUT PERHAPS IT WAS ONLY THE SOUND OF HIS CHATTERING TEETH...

35

Chapter IV

mr. Badger—

YES, YES! ALL RIGHT! I'M COMING!!

BANG BANG BANG

RING RING RING

GRUMBLE... WHO'D BE DISTURBING FOLKS WITH SUCH A RACKET? ESPECIALLY IN THE MIDDLE OF THE NIGHT!!

I'M COMING, I SAID! SAUSAGES AND SWEET BREAD!

RING RING

BANG BANG BA

REALLY. NO ONE HAS MANNERS ANY LONGER! MUMBLE.

SPLATC

?!!

SPLITCH

YOU DRATTED SCAMPS! I'LL GET YOU. SNOWMEN!!! ONLY RABBITS WOULD PLAY SUCH IDIOTIC PRANKS!!!...

ATCHOO!

?!!

WHO... WHO DID THAT?

...I DID...

SNIF...

RAT! DEAR OLD RATTY! AND HIS FRIEND MOLE, POTATOES AND FILET OF SOLE! WHAT AN IDEA TO BE STROLLING ABOUT THE WILD WOOD IN THIS WEATHER! HAVE YOU GOTTEN AS CRAZY AS TOAD?

AH! ATCH OO!

OOK!

BUT COME IN AND GET WARMED UP...

THE BADGER LED THEM DOWN A MAZE-LIKE PASSAGE WHICH WAS CRUDE AND GLOOMY, IF NOT DECIDEDLY SHABBY.

FINALLY, A STOUT OAKEN DOOR OPENED ON TO THE KITCHEN. THE FEELING THAT CAME FROM THIS PLACE WAS NOT ONE OF MANY AMENITIES, BUT OF COMFORTABLENESS. IT SEEMED LIKE NOTHING FROM THE WORLD OUTSIDE COULD TROUBLE THE PEACEFUL SECURITY OF THIS PLACE.

COME IN... I'M GOING TO MAKE SOMETHING HOT FOR YOU...

HOW FAR AWAY THE FEARS OF THE WILD WOOD SEEMED NOW...

UPON SEEING HIS FRIENDS DINING SO HEARTILY, THE BADGER COULDN'T REPRESS A SMALL, DELIGHTED SMILE.

WOULD YOU TELL ME WHAT HAPPENED TO YOU?

THE RAT AND THE MOLE BEGAN TO TELL THEIR STORY. IT WASN'T EASY TO FOLLOW, BECAUSE BOTH OF THEM WERE SPEAKING AT THE SAME TIME, AND WITH THEIR MOUTHS FULL. ALSO, YOU HAD TO WATCH OUT FOR ANY FLYING SPIT.

THE BADGER DIDN'T MIND THAT SORT OF THING. FOR HIM, GOOD MANNERS WEREN'T A MATTER OF "NO ELBOWS ON THE TABLE" OR "NO PICKING YOUR NOSE."

HE LISTENED TO THEM ATTENTIVELY, CONTENTING HIMSELF TO NOD GRAVELY AT INTERVALS IN THE STORY. THE BADGER DIDN'T MAKE JUDGMENTS ABOUT PEOPLE OR THINGS.

HE OBSERVED. THAT'S ALL.

THE MOLE BEGAN TO FEEL VERY FRIENDLY TOWARDS HIM.

WHEN SUPPER WAS FINISHED AT LAST, THEY GATHERED AROUND THE HEARTH, ONE SIPPING TEA, ANOTHER BRANDY.

HOW'S OLD TOAD GOING ON?

OH, FROM BAD TO WORSE...

WHAT'S GOING ON?

THE POOR FELLOW IS STILL CRAZY ABOUT CARS!! HE'S ALREADY WRECKED 6. NO, 7!!! THAT COACH-HOUSE OF HIS IS PILED UP WITH FRAGMENTS OF MOTOR-CARS...

THE COACH-HOUSE... SLURP... AND THE STABLES, TOO!

NOT COUNTING THE REPAIR BILLS, THE FINES AND THE STAYS IN THE HOSPITAL...HE'LL END UP KILLING HIMSELF OR BEING RUINED!

WORSE, MAYBE EVEN BOTH!!

HMM.

WELL THEN, WE CAN'T LET HIM GO ON LIKE THAT, EVEN IF HE IS A TOAD. AS SOON AS THE WEATHER IMPROVES, WE'LL TAKE HIM INTO HAND...

...WON'T WE, RAT?

I SAID: WON'T WE?

HMM?...NO...I...I WASN'T ASLEEP...

THE BADGER WAS RIGHT. FOR THE MOMENT, THEY COULDN'T DO ANYTHING... DURING THE WINTER, THE LIVES OF THE SMALL ANIMALS SLOWED DOWN. LUCKILY, CARS DID ALSO.

AFTER MAKING FUN OF RAT'S BRANDY-INDUCED DROWSINESS, OUR FRIENDS DECIDED IT WAS TIME TO GO TO BED. BADGER LED THEM TO THEIR ROOM.

THE ROOM ALSO SERVED AS A LOFT. IT WAS SCENTED BY THE AUTUMN FRUITS STORED THERE.

AS FOR THE LINENS, THOUGH A BIT COARSE, THEY WERE CLEAN AND LAVENDER SCENTED. THE MOLE AND THE WATER RAT WERE NOT SLOW ABOUT TUMBLING IN BETWEEN THEM WITH CONTENTMENT (AND ALSO WITH A GOOD FOOT-WARMER!).

THE NEXT DAY, THE MOLE AND THE RAT AWOKE VERY LATE THAT MORNING. BUT WHAT DOES THE WORD "MORNING" MEAN WHEN YOU LIVE UNDERGROUND? I ASK YOU!

MM?...

WHAT I LIKE ABOUT WAKING UP IS BREAKFAST! LAST ONE TO THE KITCHEN IS A NINNY...

I WON...

!

WELL, WELL, WHAT'S GOING ON HERE?

WE GOT LOST, SIR...THIS MORNING, MOTHER INSISTED WE GO TO SCHOOL DESPITE THE WEATHER. AND OF COURSE WE GOT A BIT LOST. AND THEN MY LITTLE BROTHER, HE STARTED GETTING SCARED...BUT THAT'S TO BE EXPECTED, HE'S YOUNG!

IT AIN'T TRUE! YOU WERE THE ONE CRYING AND SAYING "MAMA" OVER AND OVER!

AT LAST WE HAPPENED UPON MR. BADGER'S HOME AND HE INVITED US TO HAVE A NICE BOWL OF MILK PUDDING TO WARM US UP.

LIAR! LIAR! YOU WERE THE ONE WHO GOT SCARED!

WHERE IS THE GOOD BADGER THEN?

HE SAID HE WAS GOING INTO HIS STUDY TO MEDITATE A LITTLE...

OHH! YOU SCAREDY-CAT! YOU'RE A BIG, FAT GOOD-FOR-NOTHING!

CAN YOU BELIEVE IT, RAT?

HE'S ALREADY WORKING... CRUNCH..YUM..WHAT AN ANIMAL THE BADGER IS!

RAT BURST OUT LAUGHING: HE WELL KNEW THAT, AT THAT VERY MOMENT, THE BADGER HAD SETTLED INTO HIS OLD ARM-CHAIR, A RED COTTON HANDKERCHIEF OVER HIS FACE, IN THE MIDDLE OF CHATTING WITH ANGELS. IN OTHER WORDS, HE WAS SNOOZING.

SUDDENLY, THE FRONT-DOOR BELL CLANGED LOUDLY...

RIIINNG

WHO COULD IT BE NOW?

RING

?

WHAT WEATHER! BRRRR

HA! THERE YOU ARE...I WAS SURE OF IT!

OTTER! WHAT A NICE SURPRISE...

WHEN I AWOKE, THE RIVER BANK WAS IN A STATE OF ALARM.

ALL THE ANIMALS WERE TALKING ABOUT YOUR DISAPPEARANCE. THE CHATTER WAS GOING FULL-STEAM, ESPECIALLY AMONG THE MOORHENS, AS YOU MIGHT GUESS!

SO I DECIDED TO GO LOOK FOR YOU. ON THE WAY, I TOLD MYSELF THAT BADGER WOULD SURELY KNOW SOMETHING, AND HERE I AM!

HMMM, I WOULDN'T AT ALL MIND HAVING A FEW SLICES OF THIS THROWN IN THE PAN...

HOW BEAUTIFUL IT WAS OUTSIDE...YOU SHOULD'VE SEEN IT! SNOW-CASTLES, SNOW-CAVERNS, BRIDGES, TERRACES, AND RAMPARTS, ENDLESS ICE-SLIDES...

HERE AND THERE GREAT BRANCHES HAD BEEN TORN AWAY BY THE WEIGHT OF THE SNOW. THE ROBINS PERCHED ON THEM IN THEIR CONCEITED WAY, PRETENDING THEY HAD DONE IT THEMSELVES.

A BIT FURTHER ON, I CAME UPON A RABBIT. YOU SHOULD HAVE SEEN HIM WHEN I PUT MY HAND ON HIS SHOULDER! HAHA! I HAD TO SMACK HIM A COUPLE OF TIMES TO KNOCK ANY SENSE INTO HIS HEAD! HAHA! THOSE RABBITS!!

THANK YOU. IF ONLY THERE WERE A FEW HERRINGS, TOO...

HE TOLD ME THAT HE'D COME ACROSS YOU YESTERDAY, MOLE, AND THAT ALL THE RABBITS WERE TALKING ABOUT YOUR... PROBLEMS.

I SCOLDED HIM HARSHLY FOR NOT HELPING YOU, HIM AND HIS FELLOWS. HE TOLD ME IF EVERYONE STAYED HOME, THERE WOULDN'T BE ANY PROBLEMS. CAN YOU BELIEVE IT?! HA! WHAT PETTY CREATURES, THOSE RABBITS!!!!

BURP!

HIC!

I DECIDED HE HADN'T HAD HIS SHARE OF SMACKS. SO I ADDED ON A FEW MORE...HA!

WELCOME ALL AND GOOD MORNING, TURKEY BREAST AND STUFFING! HOW ARE ALL OF YOU DOING TODAY?

41

IT'LL SOON BE LUNCH TIME. ARE YOU STAYING WITH US, OTTER?

SURE. ESPECIALLY SINCE THE SIGHT OF THOSE YOUNG HEDGEHOGS STUFFING THEMSELVES WITH FRIED HAM HAS MADE ME A BIT HUNGRY!

AS FOR YOU, YOU NEED TO BE ON YOUR WAY. YOUR MOTHER WILL BE WORRIED.

HERE.

OH, THANKS.

GOOD-BYE, SIRS.

GOOD LITTLE FELLOWS. I'M NOT FOOLED BY THEIR EXCUSE FOR SKIPPING SCHOOL, BUT THEY'RE SO NICE!

RAT, YOU'LL SERVE US SOME CIDER WHILE I SET THE TABLE?

BADGER EXCELLED IN THOSE SIMPLE, BUT COPIOUS, MEALS WHICH SIMMER CLEVERLY FOR HOURS ON THE CORNER OF THE STOVE SUCH AS BEEF CASSEROLES, STEWS, GOULASHES, AND SOUPS.

AND WHILE THE RAT AND THE OTTER RIVALED THE MOORHENS WITH ALL OF THEIR RIVER-NEWS, RUMORS AND GOSSIP, THE MOLE CONGRATULATED HIS HOST ON HOW COMFORTABLE AND SAFE HIS HOME WAS.

THANK YOU. THAT'S WHAT I SAY, THERE'S NO SECURITY OR PEACE EXCEPT UNDERGROUND.

LOOK AT RAT'S HOUSE: A COUPLE OF FEET OF FLOOD-WATER AND HE'S HOMELESS!

?

AND TOAD! A FIRE, AND EARTHQUAKE, AND CRASH! NO MORE TOAD HALL! NO, I'M TELLING YOU, UP THERE OUT OF DOORS, IS ONLY GOOD ENOUGH TO ROAM ABOUT IN.

AND FOR THE RABBITS!

YES. YOU ONLY PROSPER UNDERGROUND!

I LIKE YOU. LET'S LEAVE THE OTHERS CHATTERING. I'M GOING TO REVEAL THE MYSTERIES OF MY DARK LAIR TO YOU.

YOU AT LEAST SEEM TO APPRECIATE MY RESIDENCE FOR WHAT IT'S WORTH.

OH, YOU'RE TOO KIND, YOU'RE EMBARRASSING ME...

HERE WE ARE!

THE BADGER LED THE MOLE INTO A MAZE OF PASSAGES, STAIRS AND VAULTED CEILINGS. DOORS AND WINDOWS OPENED ONTO OTHER ROOMS, AND ROOMS ONTO YET OTHERS ...EVERYTHING WAS CRAMMED WITH ALL SORTS OF STORAGE. THERE WAS ENOUGH THERE TO HOLD OUT FOR YEARS OR LONGER.

WELL?

43

IT...IT'S ASTONISHING?! YOU DID ALL THIS...

...ALL ALONE?! HAHA! I WOULD HAVE BEEN INCAPABLE, HAM AND PINNEAPPLE! NO. IT WAS THERE BEFORE. BEFORE IT WAS FULL OF EARTH AND ROOTS. BEFORE IT WAS THE WILD WOOD.

IT WAS PEOPLE WHO BUILT IT. A CITY THEY BELIEVED TO BE ETERNAL...

BUT... WHAT HAPPENED?

FAMINES, WARS, OR SIMPLY THE WEAR OF TIME, WHO CAN SAY? THINGS, LIKE FOLKS, HAVE A BIRTH, A LIFE, A DEATH. THE INHABITANTS WENT AWAY AND THE CITY DIED. IT'S THE WAY IT IS, IT'S LIFE.

AND THEN THE WINDS, THE RAIN, THE YEARS DEFEATED THESE MONUMENTS TO ETERNITY. THE BRAMBLES AND THE TREES GREW UP, THE DITCHES FILLED IN, THE BUILDINGS COLLAPSED, AND EVERYTHING LEVELED OFF...

LITTLE BY LITTLE, THE WILD WOOD WAS BORN, AND THE ANIMALS TOOK UP QUARTERS.

WITH ALL THE USUAL LOT, GOOD, BAD, AND INDIFFERENT. I'M ATTACKING NO ONE. IT TAKES ALL SORTS TO MAKE A WORLD. WE ALL LIVE BECAUSE OF AND FOR THE OTHERS. THAT'S ALL.

SO, TOMORROW, I'LL PASS THE WORD ROUND SO YOU CAN GET ABOUT WITH NO FURTHER TROUBLE.

THE MOLE WOULD HAVE NEVER THOUGHT THE BADGER TO BE SO TALKATIVE. BUT HOW INTERESTING IT HAD ALL BEEN! THE BADGER HAD THE ABILITY TO MAKE YOU FEEL THE REASONS BEHIND THINGS. LIKE THERE WAS AN UNCHANGING ORDER WHICH NONE OF OUR MISERABLE, FRENETIC EFFORTS COULD ALTER...

ENOUGH! I CAN'T TAKE IT ANYMORE!!

44

WHAT'S WRONG WITH RAT?

ALL OF A SUDDEN, THE GOOD SIR GOT UPSET ON US. HE NEEDS SOME FRESH AIR, OPEN SPACE AND DAYLIGHT!

HE FEELS LIKE THE RIVER IS GOING TO DISAPPEAR WITHOUT HIM, OR SOMETHING LIKE THAT!

EXCUSE ME, BADGER, BUT, AS THEIR NAME SUGGESTS, WATER RATS ARE NOT REALLY MADE TO LIVE UNDERGROUND...

I UNDERSTAND, MY FRIEND, AND I'M NOT ANGRY AT YOU. YOU ARE WHAT YOU ARE.

FINE. TIME TO LEAVE! I'LL COME ALONG WITH YOU.

THAT WAY, IF THERE'S A HEAD THAT NEEDS TO BE PUNCHED, I'LL BE THERE TO RENDER SERVICE!

YOU NEEDN'T FRET ABOUT CROSSING THE WILD WOOD. MY PASSAGES RUN ALL THE WAY TO THE EDGE OF THE WOOD, AND EVEN BEYOND!

FOLLOW ME...

ALL THE SAME, GENTLEMEN, I'D ASK YOU TO KEEP MY SECRET...

I PROMISE!

...I'D RATHER MY SHORT CUTS REMAIN UNKNOWN.

CROSS MY HEART...

I SWEAR.

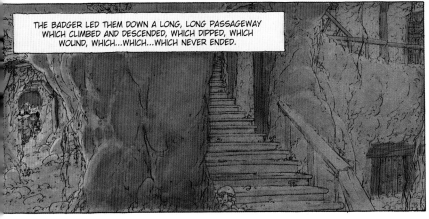

THE BADGER LED THEM DOWN A LONG, LONG PASSAGEWAY WHICH CLIMBED AND DESCENDED, WHICH DIPPED, WHICH WOUND, WHICH...WHICH...WHICH NEVER ENDED.

AT LAST, DAYLIGHT BEGAN TO SHOW THROUGH THE TANGLED GROWTH HIDING THE OPENING.

AFTER BRIEF, BUT WARM "GOOD-BYES," THE BADGER AGAIN TOOK ON HIS AIR OF THE OLD, SOLITARY CURMUDGEON, MAKING THE CAMOUFLAGE OF HIS PASSAGE LOOK AS NATURAL AS POSSIBLE, WHILE OUR FRIENDS MOVED ON ACROSS THE FIELDS GOING TOWARDS THE RIVER.

GRUMBLE

WATCH OUT, MOLE, YOU'RE GOING TO FALL...

FLATCH

PAUSING AT THE TOP OF THE HILL, THEY LOOKED BACK AND CONTEMPLATED THE SOMBER, MENACING MASS OF THE WILD WOOD AGGRESSIVELY CONTRASTING THE IMMACULATE FIELDS.

PEET

THE MOLE HESITATED A WHILE LONGER. HE DREAMT OF LIFE UNDERGROUND, HOW WELL OFF ONE WAS THERE, FAR FROM HUBBUB AND WORRIES, FAR FROM THE RUSH OF THE WORLD.

OF COURSE, ONE DIDN'T EXPERIENCE GREAT PASSIONS THERE, BUT ONE COULD FIND ALL SORTS OF SMALL ADVENTURES.

46

Chapter Ⅴ

Home sweet home—

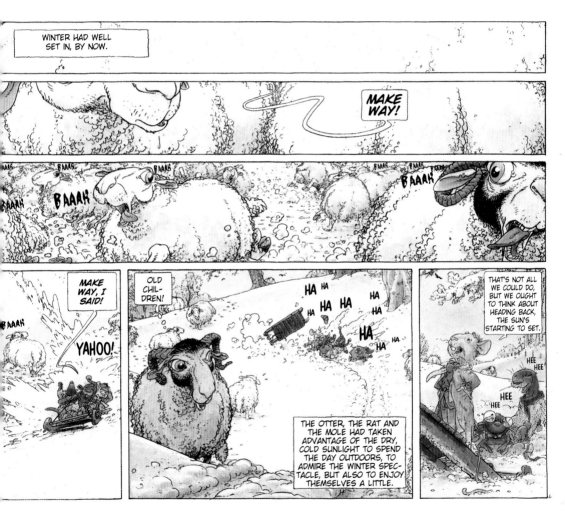

WINTER HAD WELL SET IN, BY NOW.

MAKE WAY!

BAAAH BAAAH BAAAH BAAAH BAAAH BAAAH BAAAH

MAKE WAY, I SAID!

YAHOO!

OLD CHILDREN!

HA HA HA HA HA HA HA HA

THAT'S NOT ALL WE COULD DO, BUT WE OUGHT TO THINK ABOUT HEADING BACK, THE SUN'S STARTING TO SET.

HEE HEE HEE HEE

THE OTTER, THE RAT AND THE MOLE HAD TAKEN ADVANTAGE OF THE DRY, COLD SUNLIGHT TO SPEND THE DAY OUTDOORS, TO ADMIRE THE WINTER SPECTACLE, BUT ALSO TO ENJOY THEMSELVES A LITTLE.

47

OKAY, HERE'S WHERE WE PART COMPANY. YOU'LL KNOW HOW TO FIND YOUR WAY?

OH, ME, I TRUST RAT...

CRAC!

OW

NO PROBLEM. I KNOW THIS PATH. WE ONLY HAVE TO FOLLOW IT...

OH, RAT! WHAT AN EXTRAORDINARY GUIDE YOU ARE.

THE RIVER

AND THEY EACH WENT THEIR WAY. THE OTTER HURRIED BECAUSE HE STILL HAD TO TEACH HIS LATEST BORN HOW TO SLIDE PRETTILY ON THE FROZEN POND.

TELL ME, RAT, ARE YOU SURE THIS IS THE RIGHT PATH?

YES, WHY DO YOU ASK?

WELL... BECAUSE IT LOOKS AS IF WE'RE COMING TO WHERE PEOPLE LIVE...

INDEED, WITHOUT THEIR NOTICING IT, THE PATH HAD BECOME A LANE, AND THE LANE A ROAD. NOW THEY WERE WALKING ON A COBBLE STONE STREET WHICH WAS LEADING THEM STRAIGHT TOWARDS A CHARMING VILLAGE.

48

DON'T WORRY...AT THIS HOUR AND AT THIS SEASON, THEY'RE ALL SITTING AROUND THE FIRE AT HOME.

AND I'M IMPATIENT TO BE DOING THE SAME!

THE ANIMALS, AS MUCH AS THEY CAN, TRY TO AVOID HUMANS. THEIR REACTIONS ARE SO UNPREDICTABLE. EITHER THEY'RE PETTING YOU, OR THEY'RE THROWING ROCKS AT YOU...GO FIGURE WHY...

OUR FRIENDS ENTER THE VILLAGE. THE RAT WAS CORRECT, THE STREETS WERE DESERTED. BUT THEN, THIS WASN'T WEATHER FOR MAN NOR BEAST. WELL, ALMOST.

GOOD EVENING, FELLOWS!

HOW ARE YOU DOING?

UH, HI.

A SNOW-CLAD SILENCE REIGNED THERE, SCARCELY DISTURBED BY THE SEVERAL, MUFFLED CONVERSATIONS WHICH FILTERED THROUGH THE HEAVY DOORS OF THE HOMES.

CHILDREN! I TOLD YOU TO GET TO BED!

THE RAT AND THE MOLE STOPPED TO WATCH THE SPECTACLE OF LIGHTED WINDOWS. IT WAS LIKE MANY SMALL THEATERS OF LIFE. THEY AMUSED THEMSELVES WITH IMAGINING A WHOLE BUNCH OF STORIES BASED ON EACH OF THE OFFERED SCENES.

HERE A FAMILY CRISIS.

THERE A LIGHT COMEDY.

THERE, TOO, THE INTIMATE CHRONICLE OF A CALM, FULFILLED LIFE.

49

FOR A TIME, THEY STAYED TO PONDER A PARROT RELAXING IN ITS FEATHERY COMFORT.

THEN A GUST OF BITTER WIND STRUCK THEM IN THE BACK OF THE NECK, ABRUPTLY WAKING THEM, AS IF FROM A DREAM.

WE'D BETTER GET GOING.

MY LEGS HURT AND MY FEET ARE COLD...

THEY PLODDED ALONG SILENTLY, EACH OF THEM LOST IN HIS OWN THOUGHTS. THEY WERE THINKING ABOUT THE HOME THEY'D RETURN TO SOON, ABOUT THE CREAK OF THE DOOR CLOSING BEHIND THEM ON THE WINTRY NIGHT, ABOUT THE CRACKLING OF THE FLAMES IN THE HEARTH...

THE MOLE FELT A SUCCESSION OF GURGLINGS RUMBLING THROUGH HIS STOMACH AT THE THOUGHT OF A HOT BOWL OF SOUP.

GURGLGURGLGLGURGLEGURRGLLGURRRGLGURGLE...

SUDDENLY, HE STOPPED DEAD IN HIS TRACKS.

A FUNNY, BIZARRE SENSATION... *IT WAS THERE!*

THERE IS NO WORD TO DESCRIBE THIS INTIMATE RELATIONSHIP BETWEEN AN ANIMAL AND HIS SURROUNDINGS, LIVING OR NOT. SOME SAY "SCENT" OR "INSTINCT." "HARMONY" WOULD BE MORE APT. BUT IT'S SO MUCH MORE.

I THINK WE NEED TO STEP UP THE PACE, MOLE...

THE MOLE HAD OFTEN WONDERED WHY NATURE HAD ENDOWED HIM WITH SUCH A NOSE. NOW HE KNEW. IT WAS FOR HIM TO FEEL AT HOME, TO SMELL THE NEARNESS OF HIS HOUSE.

SNIF
SNIF

HEY! I'M TALKING TO YOU!

HIS DEAR LITTLE HOUSE. WHICH HE'D MADE WITH HIS OWN PAWS, HOLE BY HOLE (IN HIS CASE, YOU REALLY COULDN'T SAY STONE BY STONE!).

IT WAS SMALL AND POORLY FURNISHED, YET IT WAS HIS AND JUST THINKING ABOUT IT MADE HIS HEART THROB.

MOLE!

WE DAREN'T STOP NOW... IT'S GETTING LATE AND THE SNOW'S COMING ON AGAIN. WE'LL COME BACK TOMORROW IF YOU LIKE.

THE MOLE'S HEART WAS TORN. ON THE ONE HAND, THE FRIENDSHIP HE'D NOT BETRAY FOR ANYTHING IN THE WORLD, AND ON THE OTHER, A BOND THAT WAS EVEN OLDER.

HIS OLD HOME WHICH MURMURED TO HIM: "STAY, STAY. LOOK AT THIS FAMILIAR SETTING...DON'T YOU FEEL YOUR ROOTS? DON'T YOU SMELL THE SOIL OF YOUR VERY EXISTENCE? WASN'T IT HERE THAT YOU DECIDED TO DIG YOUR HOLE? STAY, I TELL YOU."

THE CHOICE WAS IMPOSSIBLE. HE HAD TO ESCAPE THE PANGS OF TEMPTATION.

IT WAS WITH AN EFFORT, AND NOT VERY DECISIVELY, THAT THE MOLE SET OFF AGAIN.

THE POOR BEAST
DIDN'T LAST LONG.

BOOHOOHOO!

WHAT IS
IT, OLD
FELLOW?

IT'S...IT'S
THERE...JUST
NOW...I...CAN SMELL
MY...HOUSE...I HAD...
I HAD A...RUSH OF
MEMORIES...AND I
WANTED...TO...GO
BACK THERE...

SNIFL...

OH, RAT, I JUST WANTED...TO
TAKE A LOOK...TO SEE IF EVERY-
THING WAS OKAY...TO SEE IF
EVERYTHING WAS STILL IN PLACE
LIKE IN MY MEMORY...AND...AND
YOU DIDN'T WAAAAANNNT TOOOO!

OH?
THAT'S
ALL?

COME
ON, LET'S
GO!

BUT...THE RIVER
IS THAT WAY...
WHERE ARE
YOU GOING?

TO YOUR
HOUSE, OF
COURSE.

OH!

IT WAS A JOY TO SEE THE
MOLE CAPERING ABOUT WITH
HIS UPLIFTED NOSE, JUMPING
ABOUT AND EXCLAIMING AT
EVERY SIGN OF THE PLACE
HE'D FOUND AGAIN.

THAT
BRANCH!
...

AND
THIS
ROCK!

I'M HOME,
RAT! I'M
HOME!

NOT THAT
ONE...THAT
ONE EITHER...
HA, MAYBE...

AFTER FINDING
HIS KEYS UNDER
A FLOWER POT,
THE MOLE FEVER-
ISHLY OPENED
THE MAIN DOOR
OF HIS HOUSE.

Mole End

THEY ENTERED AN
INTERIOR GARDEN
DECORATED IN A STYLE
WHICH, FORTUNATELY,
WAS THE MOLE'S
ALONE. NEVERTHELESS
IT EXUDED A STRONG
FEELING OF SIMPLICITY
AND KINDNESS.

HEY? YOU
HAVE A
GRASS
ROLLER?

YES, I CAN'T STAND
THOSE LITTLE ANIMALS
WHO MAKE HOLES AND
LITTLE HILLS IN THE
FLOWERS...YOU KNOW?

NEXT THEY WENT INTO THE DWELLING PROPER... WELL...WHEN I SAY "PROPER"...

THE MOLE WAS SUDDENLY ASHAMED.

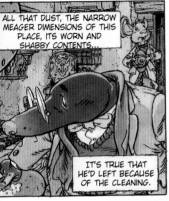

ALL THAT DUST, THE NARROW MEAGER DIMENSIONS OF THIS PLACE, ITS WORN AND SHABBY CONTENTS...

IT'S TRUE THAT HE'D LEFT BECAUSE OF THE CLEANING.

THE MOLE WOULD HAVE LIKED TO HAVE SUNK INTO THE GROUND, IF HE'D NOT ALREADY DONE SO. HE FOUND HIS HOME TO BE DISMAL AND WRETCHED COMPARED TO HIS FRIENDS'.

SPLENDID! WHAT A SURPRISE!

THESE LITTLE SLEEPING-BUNKS ARE QUITE CLEVER!

IT'S GREAT WHAT YOU MANAGE TO DO IN SUCH A SMALL SPACE! AND WHAT A CHARMING RESULT!

DO YOU THINK SO? BUT... THE DUST?

PISH TOSH! A FEW STROKES OF THE FEATHER-DUSTER AND YOU WON'T SEE IT!

IT WILL BE WON-DER-FUL.

ENCOURAGED BY THESE WORDS, THE MOLE SET TO CLEANING, AIDED BY THE RAT. LESS THAN THREE HOURS LATER, THEY'D FINISHED.

ONE HOUR OF DUSTING.

IT'S TRUE, IT'S BETTER...BUT I'M A SORRY HOST, I HAVE NOTHING TO OFFER YOU...

WHAT ARE YOU SAYING? LOOK WHAT I FOUND!

SARDINES IN OIL

IT WAS A PALTRY MEAL, BUT SHARED WITH HIS FRIEND, THE MOLE WAS SURE IT WOULD BE THE BEST OF FEASTS.

NOC NOC NO NOC NO NOC

YOU EXPECTING SOMEONE?

I DON'T THINK SO...

IT'S COMING FROM UPSTAIRS... I'LL GO SEE.

WAIT FOR ME.

1, 2...

VILLAGERS ALL, THIS FROSTY TIDE, LET YOUR DOORS SWING OPEN WIDE, THOUGH WIND MAY FOLLOW, AND SNOW BESIDE, YET DRAW US IN BY YOUR FIRE TO BIDE; HERE WE STAND IN THE COLD AND THE SLEET, BLOWING FINGERS AND STAMPING FEET, COME FROM FAR AWAY YOU TO GREET YOU BY THE FIRE AND WE IN THE STREET BIDDING YOU JOY IN THE MORNING!

"IF THE SINGERS HAVE SUNG WELL, AND BROUGHT JOY ON THIS NOEL, OPEN YOUR DOORS FOR JUST A SPELL. LET THEM IN TO WARM THEIR FEET, ON THIS CHRISTMAS AS YOU MEET, AND GIVE THEM A GOOD, RED BEET!"

IT'S VERY PRETTY. VERY PRETTY. HOW CUTE THEY ARE! EVERY YEAR THEY GO SINGING FOR TREATS...

COME IN, BOYS, COME IN.

TELL ME, ARE THERE ANY SHOPS OPEN AROUND HERE?

YES, SIR. MR. DORMOUSE'S IS. HE'S AN INSOMNIAC.

THEN HERE'S WHAT YOU'LL DO...

WAIT...WHY THE "BEET"?

I COULDN'T THINK OF ANYTHING THAT RHYMED WITH "MEET"...

YOU'LL TELL ME THAT I COULD HAVE CHANGED THE WORD "NOEL." I COULD HAVE SAID "EASTER." I'D HAVE MADE IT RHYME WITH "ROASTER." BUT IT'S CHRISTMAS. SO I DIDN'T.

THAT'S FINE. GO.

54

AND WHILE THE RAT MULLED SOME CIDER WITH A BIT OF LEMON TO GO ALONG WITH THE COOKIES, THE MOLE TOOK CARE OF THE CHILDREN.

RAT, DO YOU KNOW THEY ALSO TELL GOOD STORIES? THIS ONE TOLD ME A VERY GOOD POEM LAST YEAR ABOUT A RED HERRING AND A BIG WHITE WALL...

COME ON, CHILD. RECITE IT TO RAT.

THE POOR FIELD-MOUSE WAS SAVED BY THE ARRIVAL OF HIS BROTHER WITH A LARGE BASKET FILLED WITH EXCELLENT PROVENDER.

INSTANTLY, THE TABLE, WHICH HAD HERETOFORE BEEN SO DESPERATELY EMPTY, WAS COVERED WITH FOOD. THE RAT TWIRLED ABOUT AND OUTDID HIMSELF SO THAT EVERYTHING WOULD GO OFF AS WELL AS POSSIBLE.

AND, IN FACT, THE MOLE HAD NEVER SPENT SUCH A NICE CHRISTMAS EVE, EVEN IF IT WEREN'T QUITE YET THE VERY DAY.

THE EVENING DREW TO A CLOSE, AND FATHER FIELD-MOUSE MIGHT START WORRYING. THE WISHES OF THE SEASON WERE WARM (THE RUM SPONGE-CAKE MIGHT HAVE HAD SOMETHING TO DO WITH IT) AND EVERYONE PROMISED TO SEE ONE ANOTHER THE NEXT YEAR.

FOR OUR FRIENDS, TOO, IT WAS TIME FOR BED.

GOOD EVENING, RAT.

GOODNIGHT, MOLE.

THERE WAS "MEAT," TOO.

HMM? WHAT?

WELL...THAT RHYMES WITH "MEET."

OOOHH, MOLE!

BEFORE SHUTTING HIS EYES, THE MOLE TOOK ONE LAST LOOK AROUND HIS HOUSE.

HE HAD THE IMPRESSION THAT ALL THESE FAMILIAR OBJECTS, THE WALLS, THE CORNERS, THE NOOKS, DOWN TO THE LEAST SHAPE OF A BEAM, ALL WERE SMILING DOWN ON HIM, WELCOMING HIM. HE TOLD HIMSELF IT WAS GOOD TO HAVE A PLACE ALL HIS OWN, A REFUGE. IT DIDN'T MATTER IF HE DIDN'T LIVE THERE OFTEN. IT WAS GOOD ENOUGH SIMPLY KNOWING THAT IT WAS THERE, EVER WELCOMING. LIKE A FRIEND.

HE TOLD HIMSELF, TOO, THAT IT WAS GOOD TO SLEEP IN A BED YOU KNOW WELL AFTER A LONG DAY RIFE WITH EMOTIONS.

HE TOLD HIMSELF ALSO, THAT HE'D HAVE TO WRITE ALL THAT DOWN IN THE LITTLE PADS AS SOON AS THEY RETURNED TO THE RIVER. AND THEN, HE TOLD HIMSELF NOTHING ELSE BECAUSE HE FELL ASLEEP.

Chapter VI

Mr. Toad—

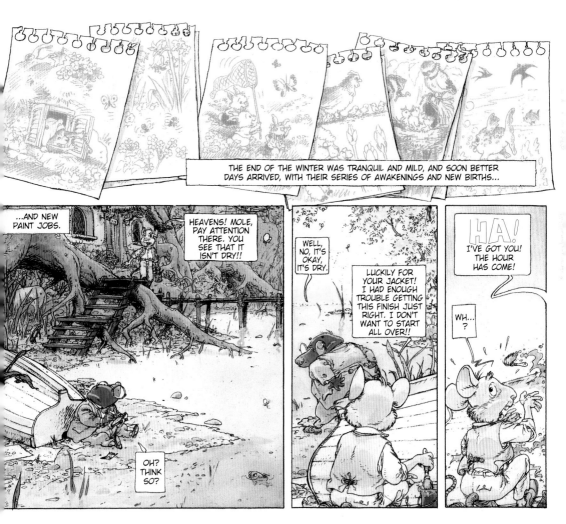

THE END OF THE WINTER WAS TRANQUIL AND MILD, AND SOON BETTER DAYS ARRIVED, WITH THEIR SERIES OF AWAKENINGS AND NEW BIRTHS...

...AND NEW PAINT JOBS.

HEAVENS! MOLE, PAY ATTENTION THERE. YOU SEE THAT IT ISN'T DRY!!

OH? THINK SO?

WELL, NO, IT'S OKAY, IT'S DRY.

LUCKILY FOR YOUR JACKET! I HAD ENOUGH TROUBLE GETTING THIS FINISH JUST RIGHT. I DON'T WANT TO START ALL OVER!!

HA! I'VE GOT YOU! THE HOUR HAS COME!

WH...?

OH! HELLO, BADGER!

WHAT DID YOU MEAN? WHAT HOUR?

"WHOSE" HOUR YOU SHOULD RATHER SAY

AND I'D TELL YOU: "TOAD'S HOUR, OF COURSE!!" DIDN'T I PROMISE YOU AS SOON AS WINTER WAS OVER, THAT WE'D TAKE CARE OF HIM?

SO, LET'S GO! THE SOONER IT'S OVER, THE BETTER! CLOVER AND HOT PEPPER!

ARE YOU REALLY SURE THAT...

COMPLETELY! SO LONG AS HIS KICKS ONLY INVOLVED HIM-SELF...BUT NOW HE'S RISKING THE LIVES OF OTHERS. HE CAN BE CRAZY, ALL RIGHT. BUT NOT IRRESPONSIBLE!

WE'RE HERE.

TOAD WILL HAVE TO LISTEN TO REA-SON!

IF IT'S NECESSARY TO BE HARSH, WE'LL BE SO!

DOES ANY ONE HAVE PIECE OF CANDY?

LOOK! HE'S STANDING ON THE STEPS.

TSSS! WHAT CLOTHING!!

HE'S MOTIONING TO US...HE'S SEEN US!

YOOHOO!

POO

POOP POOP POOP POOP POOP

PSHEE... HONK! WATCH OUT!

POOP POOP POOF

YOU ASPHALT BEAUTY!

YOU PAVEMENT JEWEL!

MY BEAUTIFUL LADY OF THE TARMAC!

58

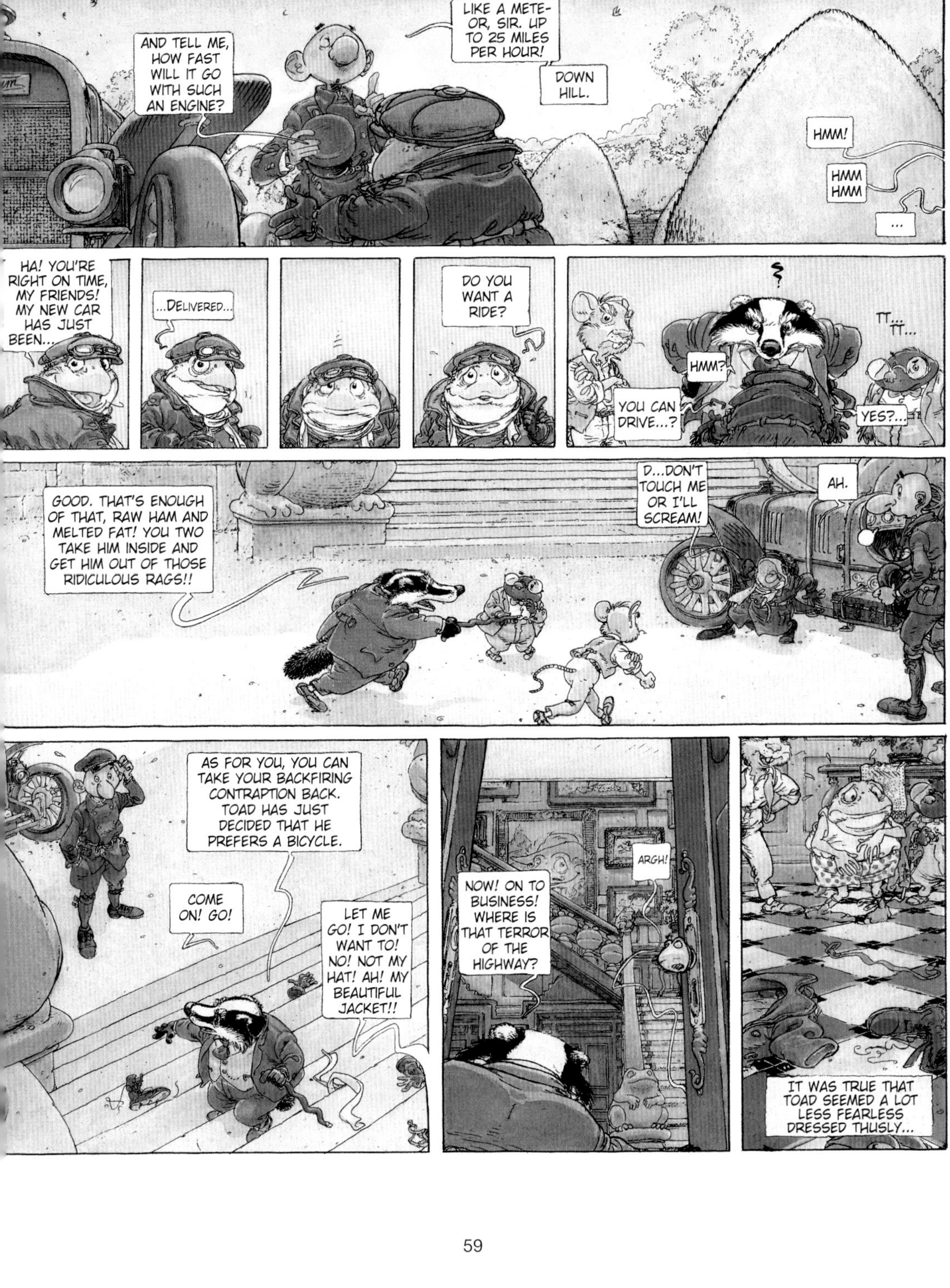
AND TELL ME, HOW FAST WILL IT GO WITH SUCH AN ENGINE?
LIKE A METE-OR, SIR. UP TO 25 MILES PER HOUR!
DOWN HILL.
HMM!
HMM HMM
...
HA! YOU'RE RIGHT ON TIME, MY FRIENDS! MY NEW CAR HAS JUST BEEN...
...DELIVERED...
DO YOU WANT A RIDE?
HMM?
TT... TT...
YOU CAN DRIVE...?
YES?...
GOOD. THAT'S ENOUGH OF THAT, RAW HAM AND MELTED FAT! YOU TWO TAKE HIM INSIDE AND GET HIM OUT OF THOSE RIDICULOUS RAGS!!
D...DON'T TOUCH ME OR I'LL SCREAM!
AH.
AS FOR YOU, YOU CAN TAKE YOUR BACKFIRING CONTRAPTION BACK. TOAD HAS JUST DECIDED THAT HE PREFERS A BICYCLE.
COME ON! GO!
LET ME GO! I DON'T WANT TO! NO! NOT MY HAT! AH! MY BEAUTIFUL JACKET!!
NOW! ON TO BUSINESS! WHERE IS THAT TERROR OF THE HIGHWAY?
ARGH!
IT WAS TRUE THAT TOAD SEEMED A LOT LESS FEARLESS DRESSED THUSLY...

COME WITH ME IN HERE, GOOD FELLOW! I HAVE A FEW THINGS TO SAY TO YOU MAN-TO-MAN!

OW

LET'S GO IN THE SMOKING-ROOM...

WOW! IT SOUNDS LIKE ORATORY!

THAT'S NO GOOD! HE'S IR-RE-DEEM-A-BLE!

SHUSH! BE QUIET! I ALREADY HAVE TROUBLE HEARING...

PSHAW!

AH. THERE, THAT'S BETTER. YES, YES... TOAD MUST BE CHOKING TO DEATH FROM SHAME, I HEAR GURGLING...

?

SO, I THINK THAT OUR FRIEND HAS UNDERSTOOD HIS LESSON. NOW TOAD, YOU'RE GOING TO REPEAT WHAT YOU JUST TOLD ME AND SWEAR THAT FROM NOW ON YOUR FOOLISHNESS IS OVER!

HMM.

I...

I'LL SWEAR NOTHING, I'M NOT SORRY FOR ANYTHING! JUST NOW, YOU TOOK ADVANTAGE OF AN EXTREMELY RARE MOMENT OF WEAKNESS ON MY PART. BUT NOW, IT'S OVER! I'M MYSELF AGAIN!!

LONG LIVE CARS! AH! DRIVING AT BREAKNECK SPEEDS!! BURNING UP THE MILES!! VROOM! POOP POOP!

THAT'S ENOUGH! LOCK HIM IN HIS ROOM!! HE'LL ONLY COME OUT WHEN HE'S GIVEN UP AND REPENTED!!!

GIVE UP? TOAD, THE BARON TADPOLE?

HA HA HA! POOP POOP! POOOT POOOT

A LITTLE PEACE AND REFLECTION WILL DO HIM A WORLD OF GOOD, RABBIT-STEW AND FIREWOOD!

POOP!

POOP!

POOP!

COME ON, TOAD! SHOW SOME PRIDE!

UNDERSTAND THAT WE'RE DOING THIS FOR YOUR OWN GOOD...

NO MORE INCIDENTS WITH THE POLICE!

NO MORE TRIPS TO THE REPAIR-SHOP!

AND NO MORE HOS-PITAL STAYS WITH THE NURSES!

YOU WON'T COME OUT AGAIN UNTIL YOU'VE BECOME A REASONABLE AMPHIBIAN!

SLAM

CLIC CLAC

OH NOOOO...

NO MORE NURSES...

ALL THE SAME... I UNDERSTAND TOAD SOMEWHAT ...OF COURSE, HE HAS A LEAD FOOT AND NO DOUBT HE NEEDS SOME CLASSES...

YEAH! AND WHAT A FOOT!

BUT AN AUTOMOBILE ALLOWS YOU TO GET AROUND MORE QUICKLY THAN ON FOOT OR EVEN IN A CARRIAGE. ALSO, IT'S LESS TIRING!

PRECISELY! IF THIS CONTRAPTION KEEPS ON, PEOPLE WILL INVADE ALL THE BEAUTIFUL PLACES! YOU'LL HAVE TO BUILD ROADS TO GO THERE AND BUILDINGS TO HOUSE THEM, THEREBY DESTROY-ING WHAT THEY CAME LOOKING FOR IN THE FIRST PLACE...

SERENITY WHILE CONTEMPLATING THE WORLD.

IN OTHER WORDS, THEY'LL MESS IT ALL UP!!

AND THEN YOU'LL HAVE TO PARK THE CARS SOMEWHERE. THEY'LL HOG THE SIDEWALKS AND THE SQUARES. CHILDREN WILL NO LONGER BE ABLE TO PLAY IN THE STREETS, AND THE PEOPLE STROLLING WILL DISAPPEAR BECAUSE IT WILL BECOME NECESSARY THAT EVERYTHING GO AS FAST AS THAT MACHINE.

SINCE PEOPLE WILL SPEND ALL THEIR TIME IN THIS ROLLING CAGE, THEY'LL LOSE THE HABIT OF SPEAKING TO ONE ANOTHER AND WILL NO LONGER UNDERSTAND ONE ANOTHER. THEN THEY'LL HATE EACH OTHER.

NO, BELIEVE ME, AS USUAL, THE HUMANS HAVE INVENTED SOMETHING THAT'S WONDERFUL, BUT ONLY THE WORSE WILL COME OF IT, AND THEY'LL RUIN THEIR LIVES AND THOSE OF OTHERS. MEANING OURS!

BRRR, HE'S EXAGGERATING A BIT, ISN'T HE?

OUR FRIENDS TOOK TURNS DAY AFTER DAY KEEPING WATCH OVER TOAD FOR THE SLIGHTEST SIGN OF RECOVERY.

SO? IS HE BETTER?

NOT REALLY... HE'S SAYING "POOP POOP" MORE AND MORE.

AT THE RATE HE'S GOING, HE'LL SOON GRADUATE TO "VROOM" AND WHY NOT "VROAR! LOOK...

?

AND HE GOES ON LIKE THAT, FASTER AND FASTER, LOUDER AND LOUDER, UNTIL HE HAS A SPASM. THEN HE COLLAPSES INTO A HEAP, EXHAUSTED, IN A CONTENTED STUPOR, UNTIL THE PAROXYSM BEGINS AGAIN...

BOOM BALANG BLENG

AAAAHHHHHH

THERE YOU HEAR

HEY! HE REMINDS ME OF A RABBIT... GO FIGURE...

WITH TIME, TOAD'S SEIZURES GREW LESS FRE-QUENT, GIVING WAY TO A STRANGE LANGUOR...

HOW ARE YOU TODAY, OLD CHAP?

HMM?

...THANKS SO VERY MUCH FOR TAKING CARE OF ME LIKE THIS, BUT I'M NOT WORTH IT...*COUGH, COUGH*...HOW BORED YOU MUST GET WHEN IT'S SURE TO BE SO PLEASANT OUTDOORS...

OH...DON'T WORRY ABOUT US. I'M ON GUARD THIS MORNING, BUT MOLE AND BADGER LEFT TO TAKE A WALK AND ENJOY THE SUNSHINE.

WHAT A SHAME THEY'VE ALREADY LEFT...I'D HAVE ASKED THEM TO FETCH THE DOCTOR...

THE WHO?

OR NO, A LAWYER RATHER. AND A PRIEST AS WELL...

A PRIEST?!!

KOF

THE RAT WAS WORRIED. THE TOAD HATED RELIGION. HE DECIDED TO THROW CAUTION TO THE WIND AND TO GO LOOK FOR THE DOCTOR.

CLACKETY, CLACKETY

IT'S TRUE THAT HE DOESN'T AT ALL SEEM WELL...NOW HE SOUNDS LIKE A CLOGGED-UP MOTOR...

"I'M NOT WORTH IT"! AS VAIN AS HE IS! IT MUST BE VERY SERIOUS!

HA HA HA HA, THE MAN HASN'T BEEN BORN WHO COULD KEEP TOAD LOCKED UP!

HEE HEE!

THE TOAD PROMPTLY DRESSED, TOOK SOME MONEY FROM A SMALL DRAWER IN THE VANITY (COME TO THINK OF IT, WHY WOULD HE NEED SUCH FURNITURE?)...

AND HERE'S THE GREAT TOAD! THE UNPARALLELED ESCAPE ARTIST! THE HOUDINI OF ANIMALS!

TA DA ♪

...AND MADE HIS ESCAPE.

LITTLE DID TOAD KNOW HOW LONG IT WOULD BE BEFORE HE WOULD SIT AT EASE AGAIN IN HIS ANCESTRAL HALL.

HA!

SO AS TO DISGUISE HIS TRAIL, HE CUT ACROSS FIELDS AT THE RISK OF HIS LIFE, CHANGED DIRECTIONS SEVERAL TIMES, TURNED, CURVED, HOPPED ALONG AND SOON, FELT HIMSELF SAFE FROM RECAPTURE.

HELLO

HELLO

HELLO

TOAD HALL

OOP

HAHA! IT WAS TOO EASY! MY GREAT BRAIN AGAINST THE BRUTE FORCE OF ONLY THREE ANIMALS! POOR THINGS, THEY DIDN'T STAND A CHANCE!

SNIF?

HELLO

AN INN! WHAT LUCK, HEROES ARE ALWAYS HUNGRY!

...AND ALSO BRING ME SOME OF THAT DELICIOUS POTATOES AU GRATIN, SOME BEEF ROUND-EYE AND CASSEROLE---DON'T BE STINGY WITH THE SAUCE---SOME RUM-CAKE AND SOME CHOCOLATE CAKE. THAT WILL BE ALL, I PREFER TRAVELING ON A LIGHT STOMACH. AH, I FORGOT...A NICE PIECE OF...

SCRITCH SCRITCH

POO Po Po Po

POOP

?

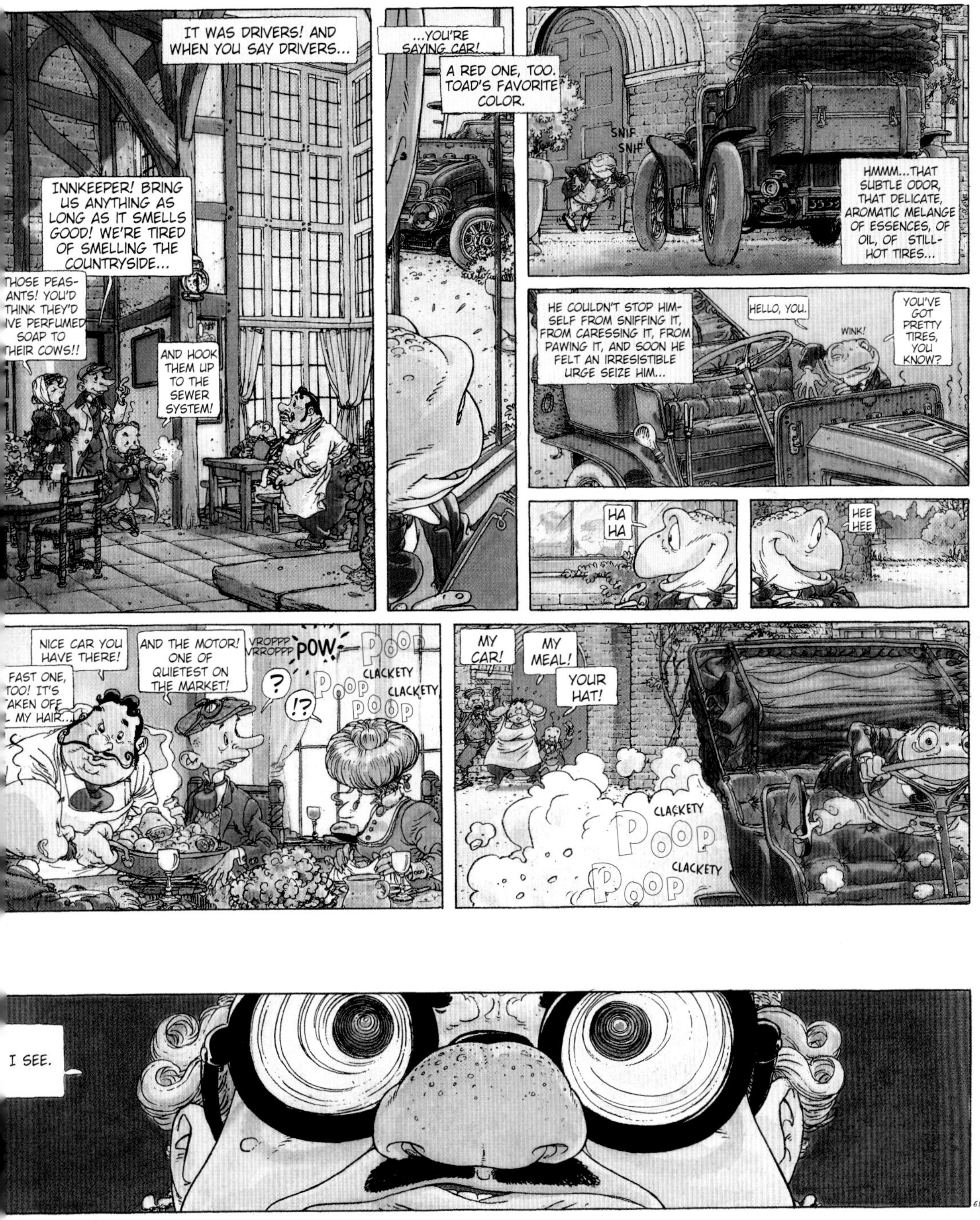
IT WAS DRIVERS! AND WHEN YOU SAY DRIVERS...
INNKEEPER! BRING US ANYTHING AS LONG AS IT SMELLS GOOD! WE'RE TIRED OF SMELLING THE COUNTRYSIDE...
THOSE PEAS-ANTS! YOU'D THINK THEY'D IVE PERFUMED SOAP TO THEIR COWS!!
AND HOOK THEM UP TO THE SEWER SYSTEM!
...YOU'RE SAYING CAR!
A RED ONE, TOO. TOAD'S FAVORITE COLOR.
SNIF
SNIF
HMMM...THAT SUBTLE ODOR, THAT DELICATE, AROMATIC MELANGE OF ESSENCES, OF OIL, OF STILL-HOT TIRES...
HE COULDN'T STOP HIM-SELF FROM SNIFFING IT, FROM CARESSING IT, FROM PAWING IT, AND SOON HE FELT AN IRRESISTIBLE URGE SEIZE HIM...
HELLO, YOU.
WINK!
YOU'VE GOT PRETTY TIRES, YOU KNOW?
HA HA
HEE HEE
NICE CAR YOU HAVE THERE!
FAST ONE, TOO! IT'S TAKEN OFF ALL MY HAIR...
AND THE MOTOR! ONE OF QUIETEST ON THE MARKET!
VROPPP VRROPPP
POW
?
!?
POOP
POOP
POOP
CLACKETY
CLACKETY
MY CAR!
MY MEAL!
YOUR HAT!
CLACKETY
POOP
CLACKETY
POOP
I SEE.
61.

WELL, GENTLE-MEN, THE MATTER SEEMS CLEAR TO ME.

IN VIEW OF ALL THE UNIMPEACHABLE WIT-NESSES, THE ACCUSED IS CLEARLY GUILTY OF ALL OF THE OFFENSES.

THE ONLY DIFFICULTY IS DECIDING THE PUNISHMENT WHICH WILL BEST PROTECT SOCIETY FROM SUCH AN INCORRIGIBLE ROGUE.

MR. CLERK?

HMM HMMM.

AFTER STUDYING THE LAWS PERTAINING TO THE DIFFERENT INFRAC-TIONS COMMITTED BY THE ACCUSED AND CAREFULLY EXAMINING THE PENALTIES LAID OUT BY THE CIVIL CODE, ACCORDING TO ARTICLES 15, 91, 135 AND 288, LINES F, H AND V, WE'VE COME TO THE FOLLOWING CON-CLUSIONS AND TALLY:

ON THE COUNT OF ORDERING FOOD WITH INSUFFICIENT FUNDS TO PAY FOR IT, WE SEN-TENCE YOU TO SIX MONTHS, WHICH IS A GIFT.

PSHAW! THAT DESERVED A LIFE SENTENCE!

WASTING SUCH A NICE CASSE-ROLE!

ON THE COUNT OF CAR-THEFT AGGRAVATED BY FLIGHT AND INAPPROPRIATE HONKING, TWELVE MONTHS, WHICH IS MILD.

HA HA

HEE HEE

CHATTER! CHATTER!

FOR HIS DANGEROUS, RECKLESS DRIVING, TWO AND A HALF YEARS, WHICH IS LENIENT.

IT'S ALL RIGHT NOW...

AS FOR HIS CHEEKY ATTITUDE TOWARDS THE LOCAL POLICE, FIFTEEN YEARS, BECAUSE OF ALL THE INFRACTIONS COMMITTED BY THE ACCUSED, THAT IS WITHOUT ARGUMENT THE WORST.

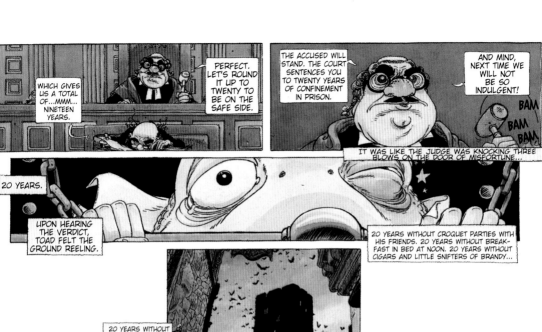

WHICH GIVES US A TOTAL OF...MMM... NINETEEN YEARS.

PERFECT. LET'S ROUND IT UP TO TWENTY TO BE ON THE SAFE SIDE.

THE ACCUSED WILL STAND. THE COURT SENTENCES YOU TO TWENTY YEARS OF CONFINEMENT IN PRISON.

AND MIND, NEXT TIME WE WILL NOT BE SO INDULGENT!

BAM BAM BAAA

IT WAS LIKE THE JUDGE WAS KNOCKING THREE BLOWS ON THE DOOR OF MISFORTUNE...

20 YEARS.

UPON HEARING THE VERDICT, TOAD FELT THE GROUND REELING.

20 YEARS WITHOUT CROQUET PARTIES WITH HIS FRIENDS. 20 YEARS WITHOUT BREAK-FAST IN BED AT NOON. 20 YEARS WITHOUT CIGARS AND LITTLE SNIFTERS OF BRANDY...

20 YEARS WITHOUT ANY FOLLIES. 20 YEARS WITHOUT ANY WHIMS. 20 YEARS WITHOUT A LIFE...

HOW COULD THE WORLD GO ON WITHOUT HIM?

WHEN HE SAW THE STOUT FORTRESS OUTLINED BEHIND THE MOB, AS QUICK TO CHASTISE THE CONDEMNED AS IT IS COMPASSIONATE WITH THE REDEEMED, TOAD TOLD HIMSELF THAT, NOW YES, IT WAS ALL OVER.

Chapter VII

The Piper at the Gates of Daw

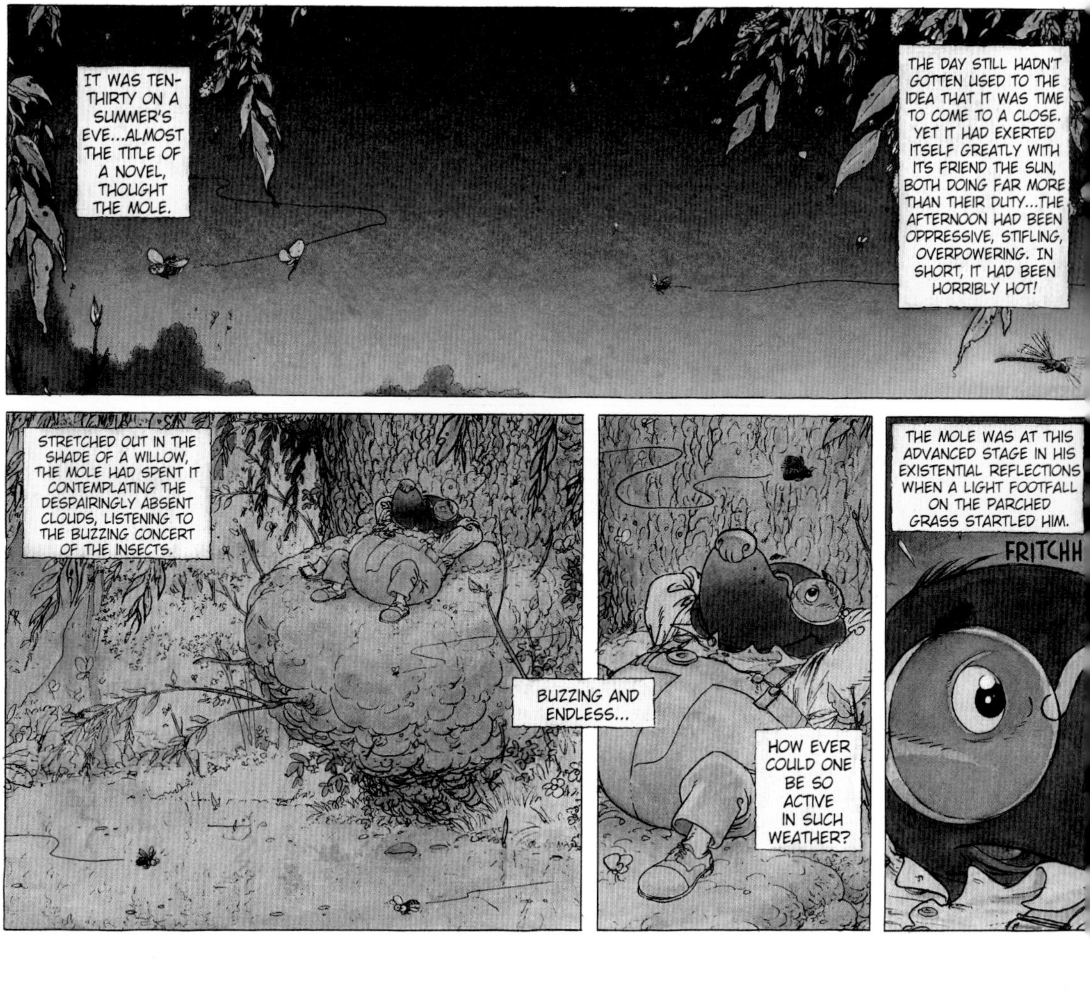
IT WAS TEN-THIRTY ON A SUMMER'S EVE...ALMOST THE TITLE OF A NOVEL, THOUGHT THE MOLE.
THE DAY STILL HADN'T GOTTEN USED TO THE IDEA THAT IT WAS TIME TO COME TO A CLOSE. YET IT HAD EXERTED ITSELF GREATLY WITH ITS FRIEND THE SUN, BOTH DOING FAR MORE THAN THEIR DUTY...THE AFTERNOON HAD BEEN OPPRESSIVE, STIFLING, OVERPOWERING. IN SHORT, IT HAD BEEN HORRIBLY HOT!
STRETCHED OUT IN THE SHADE OF A WILLOW, THE MOLE HAD SPENT IT CONTEMPLATING THE DESPAIRINGLY ABSENT CLOUDS, LISTENING TO THE BUZZING CONCERT OF THE INSECTS.
BUZZING AND ENDLESS...
HOW EVER COULD ONE BE SO ACTIVE IN SUCH WEATHER?
THE MOLE WAS AT THIS ADVANCED STAGE IN HIS EXISTENTIAL REFLECTIONS WHEN A LIGHT FOOTFALL ON THE PARCHED GRASS STARTLED HIM.
FRITCHH

RAT! YOU SCARED ME...

SO? ANY NEWS ABOUT TOAD?

WHEW. WHAT A HEAT-WAVE!

YES, I DIDN'T EVEN HAVE THE ENERGY TO SKETCH ON MY PADS TODAY!

ACCORDING TO OTTER, WHO'S CONSULTED AN EXPERT, THERE'S NOTHING TO BE DONE FOR NOW...

20 YEARS IS A LONG TIME! ESPECIALLY FOR A FROG!

WELL...AT LEAST HE'S WHERE IT'S COOL.

LETS TAKE THE TUNNEL INSTEAD. THE HOUSE IS STILL FULL OF THIS AFTERNOON'S HEAT.

YOU STAYED FOR SUPPER, OF COURSE?...

SIMPLY HAD TO. HE'D HAVE TAKEN IT AS AN INSULT AND HIS WIFE AS A CRITICISM OF HER COOKING! YOU KNOW HOW SENSITIVE THEY ARE!

THE MEAL WAS EXCELLENT NEVERTHELESS. BUT I COULD SEE SOMETHING WAS WRONG... WHEN I WAS READY TO GO, THE OTTER INSISTED ON COMING OUT WITH ME, SAYING "STRETCHING MY LEGS IS GOOD FOR DIGESTION." EXCEPT, ONCE HE WAS OUTSIDE, HE WAS HUNTING EVERYWHERE, HIGH AND LOW.

OH.

WAS HE EXPECTING SOMEONE?

YOU GUESSED IT. LITTLE PORTLY, HIS BABY, IS MISSING AGAIN.

OWEE!

THIS TIME IT'S SERIOUS! NO ONE HAS SEEN HIM FOR TWO DAYS...

65

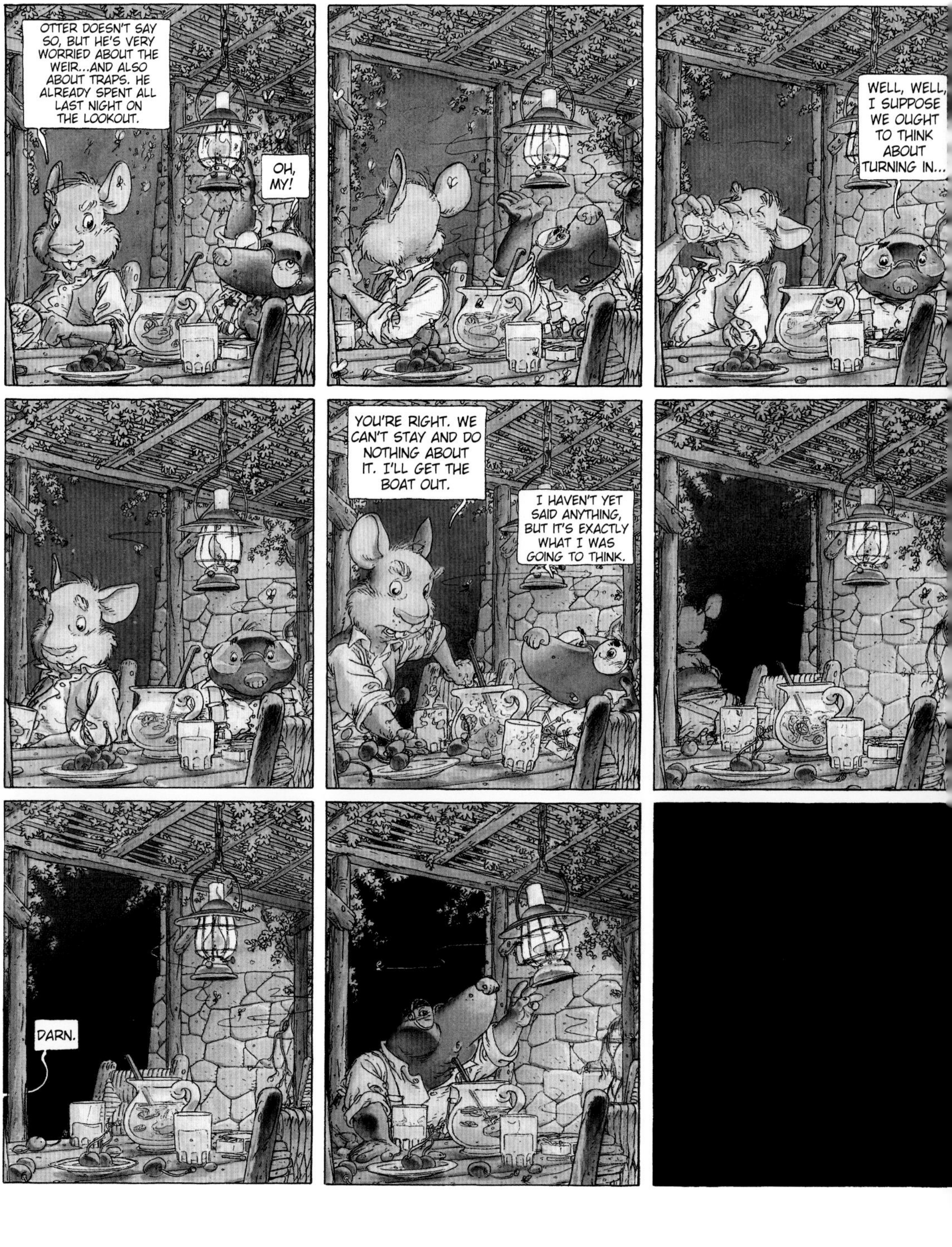
OTTER DOESN'T SAY SO, BUT HE'S VERY WORRIED ABOUT THE WEIR...AND ALSO ABOUT TRAPS. HE ALREADY SPENT ALL LAST NIGHT ON THE LOOKOUT.
OH, MY!
WELL, WELL, I SUPPOSE WE OUGHT TO THINK ABOUT TURNING IN...
YOU'RE RIGHT. WE CAN'T STAY AND DO NOTHING ABOUT IT. I'LL GET THE BOAT OUT.
I HAVEN'T YET SAID ANYTHING, BUT IT'S EXACTLY WHAT I WAS GOING TO THINK.
DARN.

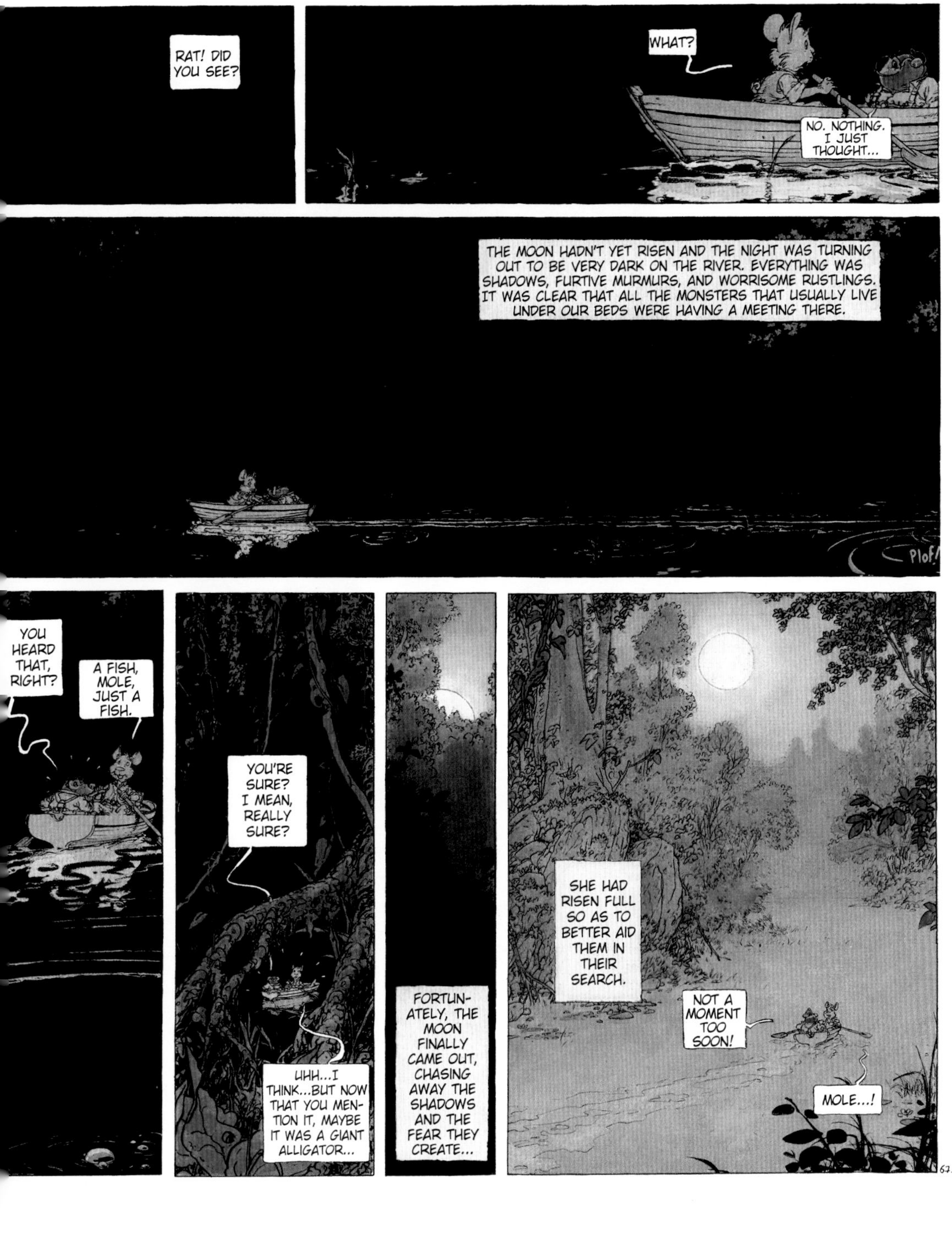
RAT! DID YOU SEE?
WHAT?
NO. NOTHING. I JUST THOUGHT...
THE MOON HADN'T YET RISEN AND THE NIGHT WAS TURNING OUT TO BE VERY DARK ON THE RIVER. EVERYTHING WAS SHADOWS, FURTIVE MURMURS, AND WORRISOME RUSTLINGS. IT WAS CLEAR THAT ALL THE MONSTERS THAT USUALLY LIVE UNDER OUR BEDS WERE HAVING A MEETING THERE.
Plof!
YOU HEARD THAT, RIGHT?
A FISH, MOLE, JUST A FISH.
YOU'RE SURE? I MEAN, REALLY SURE?
UHH...I THINK...BUT NOW THAT YOU MENTION IT, MAYBE IT WAS A GIANT ALLIGATOR...
FORTUNATELY, THE MOON FINALLY CAME OUT, CHASING AWAY THE SHADOWS AND THE FEAR THEY CREATE...
SHE HAD RISEN FULL SO AS TO BETTER AID THEM IN THEIR SEARCH.
NOT A MOMENT TOO SOON!
MOLE...!

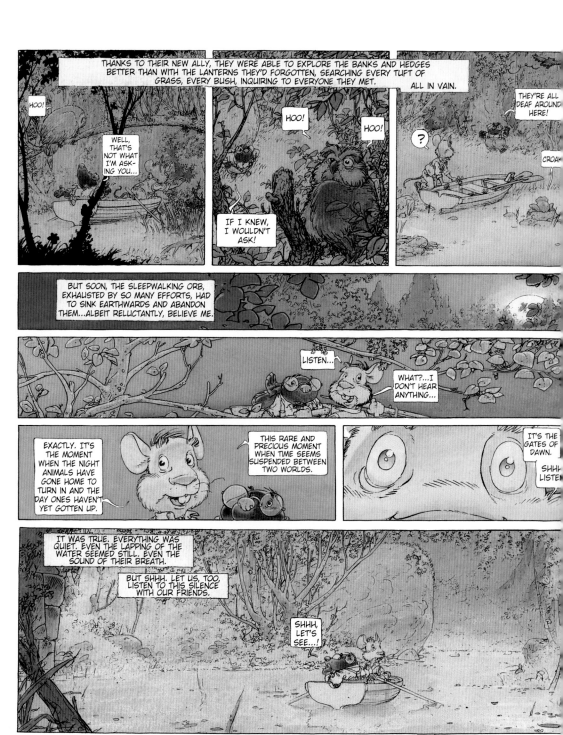

THANKS TO THEIR NEW ALLY, THEY WERE ABLE TO EXPLORE THE BANKS AND HEDGES BETTER THAN WITH THE LANTERNS THEY'D FORGOTTEN, SEARCHING EVERY TUFT OF GRASS, EVERY BUSH, INQUIRING TO EVERYONE THEY MET. ALL IN VAIN.

HOO!

WELL, THAT'S NOT WHAT I'M ASK- ING YOU...

HOO!

HOO!

IF I KNEW, I WOULDN'T ASK!

?

THEY'RE ALL DEAF AROUND HERE!

CROAK

BUT SOON, THE SLEEPWALKING ORB, EXHAUSTED BY SO MANY EFFORTS, HAD TO SINK EARTHWARDS AND ABANDON THEM...ALBEIT RELUCTANTLY, BELIEVE ME.

LISTEN...

WHAT?...I DON'T HEAR ANYTHING...

EXACTLY. IT'S THE MOMENT WHEN THE NIGHT ANIMALS HAVE GONE HOME TO TURN IN AND THE DAY ONES HAVEN'T YET GOTTEN UP.

THIS RARE AND PRECIOUS MOMENT WHEN TIME SEEMS SUSPENDED BETWEEN TWO WORLDS.

IT'S THE GATES OF DAWN.

SHHH LISTE

IT WAS TRUE. EVERYTHING WAS QUIET. EVEN THE LAPPING OF THE WATER SEEMED STILL. EVEN THE SOUND OF THEIR BREATH.

BUT SHHH. LET US, TOO, LISTEN TO THIS SILENCE WITH OUR FRIENDS.

SHHH, LET'S SEE...!

72

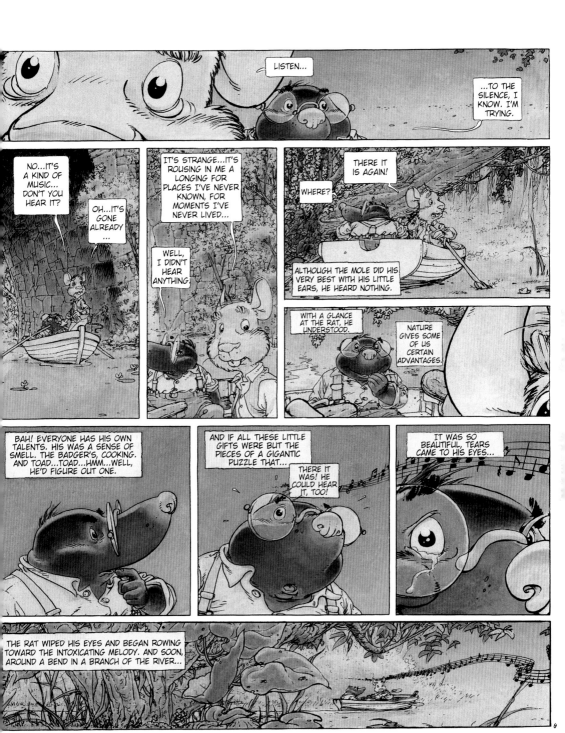

LISTEN...

...TO THE SILENCE, I KNOW. I'M TRYING.

NO...IT'S A KIND OF MUSIC... DON'T YOU HEAR IT?

OH...IT'S GONE ALREADY...

IT'S STRANGE...IT'S ROUSING IN ME A LONGING FOR PLACES I'VE NEVER KNOWN, FOR MOMENTS I'VE NEVER LIVED...

WELL, I DIDN'T HEAR ANYTHING.

THERE IT IS AGAIN!

WHERE?

ALTHOUGH THE MOLE DID HIS VERY BEST WITH HIS LITTLE EARS, HE HEARD NOTHING.

WITH A GLANCE AT THE RAT, HE UNDERSTOOD.

NATURE GIVES SOME OF US CERTAIN ADVANTAGES.

BAH! EVERYONE HAS HIS OWN TALENTS. HIS WAS A SENSE OF SMELL. THE BADGER'S, COOKING. AND TOAD...TOAD...HMM...WELL, HE'D FIGURE OUT ONE.

AND IF ALL THESE LITTLE GIFTS WERE BUT THE PIECES OF A GIGANTIC PUZZLE THAT...

THERE IT WAS! HE COULD HEAR IT, TOO!

IT WAS SO BEAUTIFUL, TEARS CAME TO HIS EYES...

THE RAT WIPED HIS EYES AND BEGAN ROWING TOWARD THE INTOXICATING MELODY. AND SOON, AROUND A BEND IN A BRANCH OF THE RIVER...

IT SEEMED TO BE COMING FROM THERE, FROM THAT SMALL ISLAND BORDERED WITH WILLOWS AND SILVERED BIRCHES. SOMETHING IRRESISTIBLE DREW THEM THERE.

THEY LANDED WITHOUT INCIDENT. THE GROUND WAS CARPETED WITH FRAGRANT FLOWERS AND SOFT, THICK MOSS.

THEY FOLLOWED A SORT OF PATHWAY BETWEEN THE WILD FRUIT-TREES. THE MOLE WAS SO AGITATED THAT HE DIDN'T EVEN THINK OF GORGING HIMSELF.

THE MUSIC HAD STOPPED. THE MOLE, TOO. EVERYTHING NOW SEEMED UTTERLY SILENT. IT SEEMED TO HIM THAT SOME TERRIBLE AND BEAUTIFUL PRESENCE WAS NEAR. SOMETHING THAT DEMANDED AWE AND RESPECT, THAT HE WOULD DOUBTLESS NEVER AGAIN SEE.

SO, SLOWLY, HUMBLY, THE MOLE DARED TO LIFT HIS EYES.

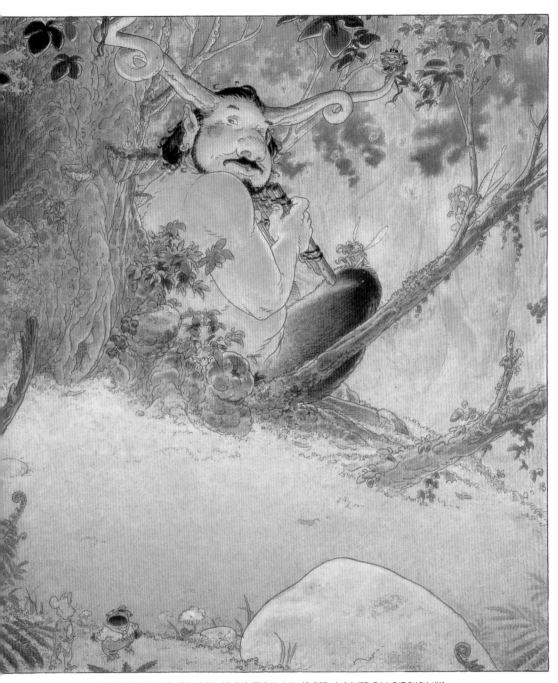

HE LOOKED IN THE VERY EYES OF THE FRIEND AND HELPER. A SHIVER RAN THROUGH HIM.

ARE YOU AFRAID?
OF HIM? O, NEVER. AND YET...
SUDDENLY THE FIRST SUNBEAM DAZZLED FORTH.
WHEN THEY WERE ABLE TO SEE AGAIN, THE VISION HAD VANISHED...
THE AIR WAS FULL OF THE CAROL OF THE BIRDS THAT HAILED THE DAWN, THE RIVER WHISPERED AS BEFORE. TIME HAD RESUMED ITS COURSE.
A BREEZE SPRUNG UP, MAKING THE POPLARS SHIVER AND SHIMMER LIKE A DOWNPOUR OF FINE PIECES OF GOLD... IT DANCED THROUGH THE LILIES AND WILD ROSES STILL COVERED IN LIGHT DEW... ...AND BLEW LIGHTLY ON THE FACES OF OUR FRIENDS, GIVING THEM THE LAST GIFT OF THE FRIEND: FORGETFULNESS.
?!
FOR IF KNOWLEDGE IS IMPORTANT, OBLIVION IS THE SOURCE OF INNOCENCE.
...
WHAT DID YOU SAY, RAT?...
...I FOR-GET...
"LEAVE THIS FROG IN PEACE"? ...

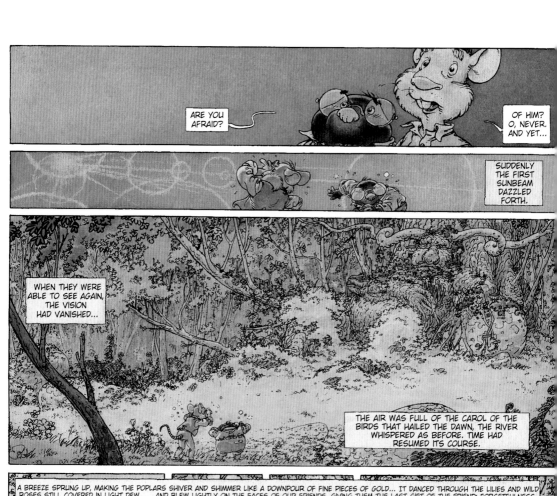

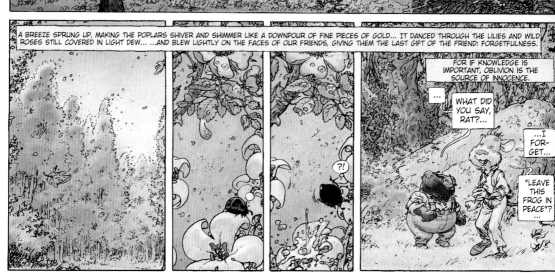

THE LITTLE ANIMALS REMAINED DAZED AND DUMBFOUNDED. THEY FELT AS THOUGH THEY HAD THE DIM AFTER-THOUGHT OF AN UNCERTAIN MEMORY...

?

IT WAS AS THOUGH THEY'D AWAKENED FROM A BEAUTIFUL DREAM, ALREADY FADING DESPITE THE STRUGGLE TO RECALL, LEAVING ONLY A PROFOUND, SERENE FEELING OF WELLBEING.

HELLO? SOME GREAT ANIMAL HAS BEEN HERE...

I WONDER WHERE HE WENT... THE ISLAND IS SO LITTLE...

HUH?! A BEAST? WHERE??

AAH! SOMETHING MOVED OVER THERE!

WHERE?

THERE, I TELL YOU!

IT SEEMS PRETTY SMALL TO HAVE LEFT SUCH BIG TRACKS...

LITTLE PORTLY!

WELL, YOU CAN BRAG THAT YOU HAD US WORRIED, YOU LITTLE SCAMP!

YOU KNOW, I WASN'T AFRAID!

I'D NEVER SEEN HIM BEFORE, BUT, I DON'T KNOW WHY, I'D HAVE RECOGNIZED HIM RIGHT AWAY.

WHILE LEAVING THE ISLAND, THE MOLE COULDN'T STOP HIMSELF FROM TURNING BACK ONE FINAL TIME, FULL OF AN INCOMPREHENSIBLE SADNESS, AND FROM CONTEMPLATING THIS PLACE THAT, HE DIDN'T KNOW WHY, WOULD ALWAYS BE PART OF HIM.

WE WON'T LINGER OVER THE INTIMACY OF THE REUNION OF FATHER AND SON, AND LIKE THE MOLE AND RAT, LET'S DISTANCE OURSELVES DISCREETLY.

SO! THERE YOU ARE?!

AND YOUR MOTHER? DID YOU THINK OF YOUR POOR MOTHER?

23.

I FEEL STRANGELY TIRED, AS IF I'D BEEN THROUGH SOMETHING EXCITING AND RATHER SPLENDID...YET NOTHING PARTICULAR HAS HAPPENED.

ME, TOO... I HAVE THE SAME FEELING...

AHHH, WHAT CALM...

DO YOU HEAR THE WIND IN THE WILLOWS? IT'S LIKE MUSIC...

HERE'S HOW IT GOES:

"LEST THE AWE SHOULD DWELL AND TURN YOUR FROLIC TO FRET YOU SHALL LOOK ON MY POWER AT THE HELPING HOUR BUT THEN YOU SHALL FORGET! HELPER AND HEALER, I CHEER SMALL WAIFS IN THE WOODLAND WET STRAYS I FIND IN IT, WOUNDS I BIND IN IT BIDDING THEM ALL FORGET!"

IT WAS A REAL SONG!...DID YOU HEAR?

HEY, RAT!

THE RAT COULDN'T RESPOND. WITH A SMILE OF MUCH HAPPINESS ON HIS FACE, HIS DEEP, REGULAR BREATHING REVEALED THAT THE RAT WAS FAST ASLEEP.

THE MOLE TOLD HIMSELF HE WOULDN'T BE LONG IN IMITATING HIM. AFTER ALL, THE BOAT KNEW ITS WAY HOME, IT WOULD KNOW HOW TO MANAGE ON ITS OWN.

Chapter VII

Toad's Adventures

ALL THAT TIME YET TO BE SPENT DEEP IN THIS DANK DUNGEON...

POOR TOAD...

AH! HOW HE REGRETTED STEALING THAT CAR AND SHOWING SO MUCH CHEEK TO THOSE FAT, RED-FACED POLICEMEN!

Z Z Z Z

YAHOO!

HEY! BETSY! WAIT UP...

SNIFF

ONE MUST, ALL THE SAME, RECOGNIZE THAT THE THEFT HAD BEEN COMMITTED WITH FLAIR, THAT THE JUDICIOUS CHOICE OF RINGING, VIVID INSULTS REVEALED A LIVELY, CULTIVATED MIND.

BETSY?

AAH!

HEH HEH

WHEN HE GOT OUT, HE'D BE OLD, STAID, INCAPABLE OF THE SLIGHTEST CAPRICE, AND WOULD BE REDUCED TO PLAYING BRIDGE WITH HIS FRIENDS...

WELL?! IT'S JUST A TOAD AFTER ALL...

I CAN'T HELP IT, SIMONE. I'VE ALWAYS HAD A FEAR OF FROGS.

NOT EVEN! HIS FRIENDS HAD SURELY ALREADY FORGOTTEN HIM...HE'D END UP ALONE, LIKE AN OUTCAST, SHUNNED BY ALL. IN RAGS. IN A DITCH. HIM, THE ONE AND ONLY TOAD!

B... BOO...

BOOHOOHOO!

WELL, I THINK YOU SHOULD TALK TO YOUR SHRINK...

THE JAILER'S DAUGHTER -RATHER SPRYER THAN HER FATHER- WAS MUCH AFFECTED BY THE MOANING OF THE TOAD. IT MUST BE NOTED THAT SHE WAS PARTICULARLY FOND OF ANIMALS AND ALREADY KEPT A FEW.

BOOHOOHWAH

GOOD LORD! I CAN'T BEAR HEARING THAT! SOMETHING MUST BE DONE!

TAKE CARE OF THAT CRAZY FROG?

IF YOU WANT, BUT THERE'S NOTHING TO BE DONE WITH HIM! I'VE ALREADY PROPOSED A SMALL UNDERSTANDING WITH HIM FOR A BIT OF MONEY....WELL, NOOO! MASTER MONEY BAGS REFUSED IT ALL!

HE'S CRAZY, HE'S CRAZY

CAW! HE'S CRAZY

I SAY...

SPPPPT

HE'S... RRRA

...HE'S CRAZY

80

WHEN SHE ENTERED, A DELICIOUS FRAGRANCE FILLED BOTH THE ROOM AND TOAD'S NOSTRILS.

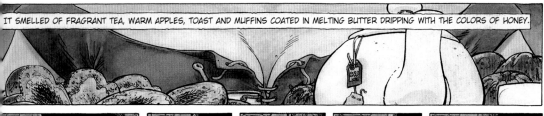

IT SMELLED OF FRAGRANT TEA, WARM APPLES, TOAST AND MUFFINS COATED IN MELTING BUTTER DRIPPING WITH THE COLORS OF HONEY.

IT WAS CLEAR! SHE WAS GOING TO TRY TO SEDUCE HIM THROUGH HIS STOMACH... A CLASSIC FEMININE TECHNIQUE...

THAT WAS MAKING LITTLE ADO OF HIS FAMOUS STRENGTH OF CHARACTER!

WHAT A CRUDE STRATAGEM! HA! NEVER WOULD A FROG WORTHY OF THE NAME LET HIMSELF BE TRAPPED SO EASILY!

KS
KSS

KSS

YUM
SCRUNCH GOBBLE
GORGE SMACK CRUNCH
BURP
GLOOP

HEE HEE

I KNEW YOU WEREN'T SO DIFFICULT...

UNTIL TOMOR-ROW?

AS THE DAYS WENT ON, THE CONVERSATIONS BECAME FREQUENT.

TELL ME ABOUT YOURSELF...

MY DEAR. ONLY MY LEGENDARY MODESTY FORBIDS ME FROM REVEALING TO YOU HOW MUCH I'M OUT OF THE ORDINARY!

LITTLE BY LITTLE, THE GIRL GREW VERY SORRY FOR THIS POOR CREATURE WHO WAS DECIDEDLY MORE RIDICULOUS THAN DANGEROUS...

TELL ME ABOUT TOAD HALL, THEN...

IT IS, WITHOUT A DOUBT, THE IDEAL RESIDENCE FOR THE EXCEPTIONAL GENTLEMAN: 38 ROOMS, KITCHENS, BATHROOMS REPLETE WITH THE LATEST, MODERN CONVENIENCE ALL IN A 16TH-CENTURY PAVILION, A GARDEN, STABLES, A VAST, SHADED, LAND-SCAPED PARK, PRIVATE ACCESS TO THE RIVER, EVERYTHING DECORATED IN THE BEST TASTE, FIVE MINUTES FROM CHURCH, POST-OFFICE, AND GOLF COURSE. SUITABLE FOR...

WHOA! I DON'T MEAN TO BUY IT! HAHA!

HEHH...

THE TOAD WAS CONVINCED THAT HIS WARM CHARM WASN'T LEAVING THE YOUNG WOMAN INDIFFERENT. BUT TOO MANY DIFFERENCES SEPARATED THEM...THERE WAS A SOCIAL GULF BETWEEN THEM THAT NOTHING COULD EVER SPAN.

BARON TADPOLE WITH SOME JAILER'S DAUGHTER... WHAT A RIDICULOUS IDEA!

ONE MORNING THE GIRL ENTERED WITH AN UNUSUALLY THOUGHTFUL AIR...

I... HMM...

I HAVE TO TELL YOU... MY AUNT IS A WASHER-WOMAN AND...

THERE, THERE, THINK NO MORE OF IT...I, TOO, HAVE SEVERAL OLD AUNTS WHO OUGHT TO BE WASHERWOMEN.

???

WON'T YOU *BE QUIET A MINUTE, TOAD?!* IT'S ABOUT YOUR ESCAPE!!

WITH A FEW WORDS, THE GIRL REVEALED HER PLAN TO HIM.

TOAD? IN PETTICOATS?

NO WAY!

COME NOW. IT'S THE ONLY WAY!

STAY HERE, I'LL BE RIGHT BACK...

HERE.

THIS IS MY OLD AUNT...

HEE HEE

WHAT?... IT'LL NEVER WORK?!!!

WE DON'T AT ALL HAVE THE SAME FIGURE,

LOOK...

AND I AM MUCH MORE ELEGANT!

HA!

HEE HEE

MY AUNT THINKS SO, TOO.

HA!

I MEAN SHE TOO THINKS SHE'S MORE ELEGANT.

HA?

TOAD HAD TO RESOLVE HIMSELF. THERE WAS NO OTHER POSSIBLE ALTERNATIVE. LIKE A GREAT LORD, HE GENEROUSLY PAID THE LARGE SUM REQUESTED BY THE OLD WOMAN.

GRMBL!

PFF.

HMPH!

ARGH!

IT WAS THEN NECESSARY TO EXCHANGE CLOTHES AND TIE UP THE OLD AUNT IN ORDER TO AVERT SUSPICION.

IT IS OKAY? NOT TOO TIGHT?

OH, AT THAT PRICE...

I TOLD YOU SO! I'M MUCH TOO ELEGANT! IT'LL BE NOTICED RIGHT AWAY...

THE TOAD PROPOSED ADDING SOME BUMPS AND BLACK EYES TO MAKE IT LOOK MORE REAL.

DON'T BE A TADPOLE. IT'S TIME TO GO.

HMM! HMM!

I'M AN EXPERT! I'M ACQUAINTED WITH SEVERAL POLICEMEN WHO CAN ATTEST TO IT...

THE ESCAPE WAS BEGINNING...

SUDDENLY...

ERH...

HELLO, DOLL! HOW 'YA DOIN'?

NO WAY TO GO BACK...

HOW ABOUT A LITTLE KISS?

EE!

THE TOAD UNDERSTOOD THE HARD LIFE OF WOMEN...HE SWORE TO NEVER AGAIN PINCH HIS NURSES' REAR-ENDS...

HEE HEE

WELL, MAYB JUST A LITTLE...

SUCH SCOUN-DRELS!

NOW, WHERE'S THE EXIT? I'M GOING TO END UP BEING SEEN...

HEY! YOU THERE!

GO ON.

HURRY UP NOW! I'M ONLY WAITING FOR YOU BEFORE SHUT-TING THE GATES!

OUT!

HMPH!! MY TEA'LL BE COLD AGAIN!

DAYLIGHT...

THE TOAD HAD ALMOST FOR-GOTTEN ITS EXISTENCE...

FREE?...

FREE!

FREE!

FREE!

FREE!

FREE!

FREE!

FREE!

FREE!

ONCE AGAIN, THE SPECTACULAR TOAD HAD ABLY TRIUMPHED OVER ADVERSITY.

WHEW! IT WAS ONLY A TRAIN...

A STATION...

WITH A LITTLE LUCK, HE'D SPEND A SNUG NIGHT IN HIS OWN BED.

A TRAIN? BUT THEN...

YES!

INDEED, THERE WAS A TRAIN. SO MUCH LUCK TRULY BORDERED ON GENIUS!

EVEN BETTER, HE HAD PLENTY OF TIME.

WELL, MAYBE NOT SO MUCH AS ALL THAT!...

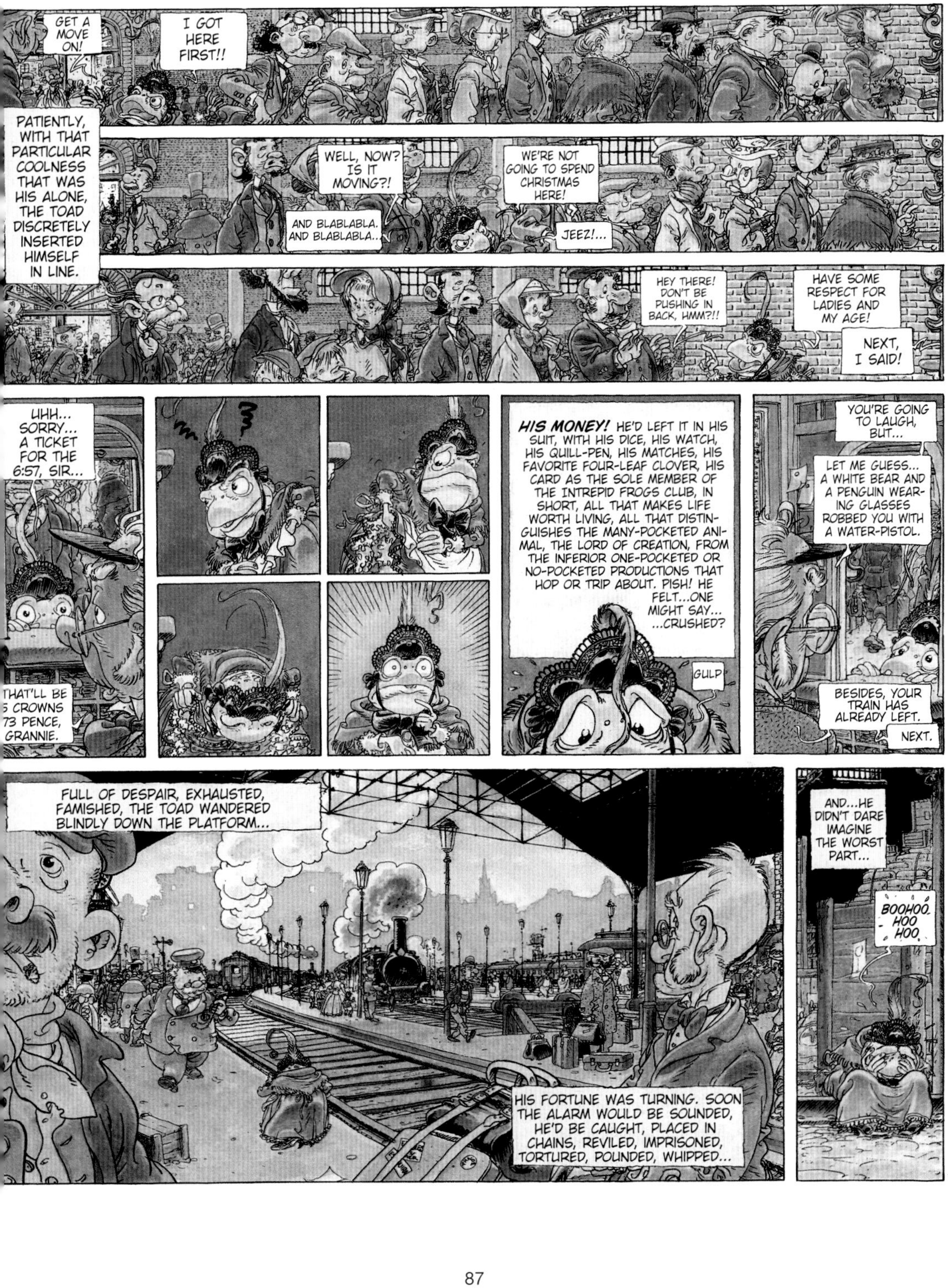

GET A MOVE ON!
I GOT HERE FIRST!!
PATIENTLY, WITH THAT PARTICULAR COOLNESS THAT WAS HIS ALONE, THE TOAD DISCRETELY INSERTED HIMSELF IN LINE.
WELL, NOW? IS IT MOVING?!
AND BLABLABLA. AND BLABLABLA...
WE'RE NOT GOING TO SPEND CHRISTMAS HERE!
JEEZ!...
HEY THERE! DON'T BE PUSHING IN BACK, HMM?!!
HAVE SOME RESPECT FOR LADIES AND MY AGE!
NEXT, I SAID!
UHH... SORRY... A TICKET FOR THE 6:57, SIR...
THAT'LL BE 5 CROWNS 73 PENCE, GRANNIE.
HIS MONEY! HE'D LEFT IT IN HIS SUIT, WITH HIS DICE, HIS WATCH, HIS QUILL-PEN, HIS MATCHES, HIS FAVORITE FOUR-LEAF CLOVER, HIS CARD AS THE SOLE MEMBER OF THE INTREPID FROGS CLUB, IN SHORT, ALL THAT MAKES LIFE WORTH LIVING, ALL THAT DISTINGUISHES THE MANY-POCKETED ANIMAL, THE LORD OF CREATION, FROM THE INFERIOR ONE-POCKETED OR NO-POCKETED PRODUCTIONS THAT HOP OR TRIP ABOUT. PISH! HE FELT...ONE MIGHT SAY... ...CRUSHED?
GULP
YOU'RE GOING TO LAUGH, BUT...
LET ME GUESS... A WHITE BEAR AND A PENGUIN WEARING GLASSES ROBBED YOU WITH A WATER-PISTOL.
BESIDES, YOUR TRAIN HAS ALREADY LEFT.
NEXT.
FULL OF DESPAIR, EXHAUSTED, FAMISHED, THE TOAD WANDERED BLINDLY DOWN THE PLATFORM...
HIS FORTUNE WAS TURNING. SOON THE ALARM WOULD BE SOUNDED, HE'D BE CAUGHT, PLACED IN CHAINS, REVILED, IMPRISONED, TORTURED, POUNDED, WHIPPED...
AND...HE DIDN'T DARE IMAGINE THE WORST PART...
BOOHOO. HOO HOO.
83

HULLO, LITTLE LADY! WHAT'S THE TROUBLE?

?!!

SO MUCH KINDNESS AND SOLICITUDE COULD NOT GO UNUSED...

MAY I HELP YOU?

O, SIR!

I JUST MISSED THE LAST TRAIN...

IT'S AWFUL AWFUL AWFUL...

WHAT WILL BECOME OF MY CHILDREN WITHOUT THEIR DEAR MOTHER?!

SNIFF!

...THEY WON'T THINK TO TAKE THEIR MEDICINE ALL ALONE, 'CAUSE, I MUST SAY, THEY ALL FELL SICK AFTER THE DEATH OF THEIR POOR FATHER, JUST AFTER OUR BELONGINGS WERE REPOSSESSED...

PLEASE IT'S TOO SAD.

I CAN'T RESIST PRETTY WOMEN IN DISTRESS... GET ON, I'LL TAKE YOU.

IT'S VERY KIND, BUT I DON'T HAVE ANYTHING TO PAY YOU...

DON'T YOU FRET...

WE'LL MAKE A DEAL.

HOW AMUSING IT SEEMED TO DRIVE A TRAIN....!

HE'D SURELY GIVE IT A TRY ONE DAY.

THIS TIME, THE TOAD COULD REALLY SMELL THE SCENT OF FREEDOM...

ATCHOO!

SOON, HE'D BE AT HIS ABODE, HIS DOMICILE, IN SHORT, HIS HOME...

THAT'S STRANGE...

?!

HE WAS ALREADY CONSIDERING HIS SUPPER, WHEN...

THERE'S A TRAIN FOLLOWING US WHEN WE SHOULD BE ALONE ON THE TRACK...

THE POLICE! HIS GOOSE WAS COOKED!

POW
POW
POW

MERCY! I LIED TO YOU.

I'M NOT THE WASHERWOMAN THAT I SEEM TO BE...I'M A DANGEROUS CRIMINAL WHO HAS JUST DAR-INGLY ESCAPED FROM THE MOST LOATHSOME, ROTTEN, NAUSE-ATING DUNGEON ON EARTH!

?

NOBODY'S PERFECT...

OH, KIND SIR! IF YOU ONLY KNEW WHAT I'VE HAD TO ENDURE!

THERE WASN'T EVEN ANY SOUR-ORANGE JAM FOR BREAKFAST...!

WHAT DID YOU DO?

OOOHHH, NOTHING VERY MUCH...I ONLY BORROWED SOMETHING WITHOUT PERMIS-SION. BUT YOU KNOW HOW PEO-PLE ARE ONCE YOU TOUCH THEIR DEAR PROPERTY!

YEP. IN ANY CASE, NO ONE GIVES ME ORDERS WHEN I'M ON MY OWN ENGINE.

ESPECIALLY THE POLICE.

NOW YOU PILE ON THE FURNACE WITH ALL THE COAL YOU CAN SHOVEL!

SIR, YES, SIR!

A PITILESS PURSUIT GOT UNDERWAY.

MMOOOO!

WELL, AREN'T WE SPOILED!

ALAS, WEIGHTED DOWN BY THE CARS, THEY DIDN'T HAVE A CHANCE.

IT'S NO USE! THEY'RE CATCHING UP!

THEN, THERE'S NO OTHER CHOICE!

HEY?!

WHAT ARE YOU DOING?!!

85

89

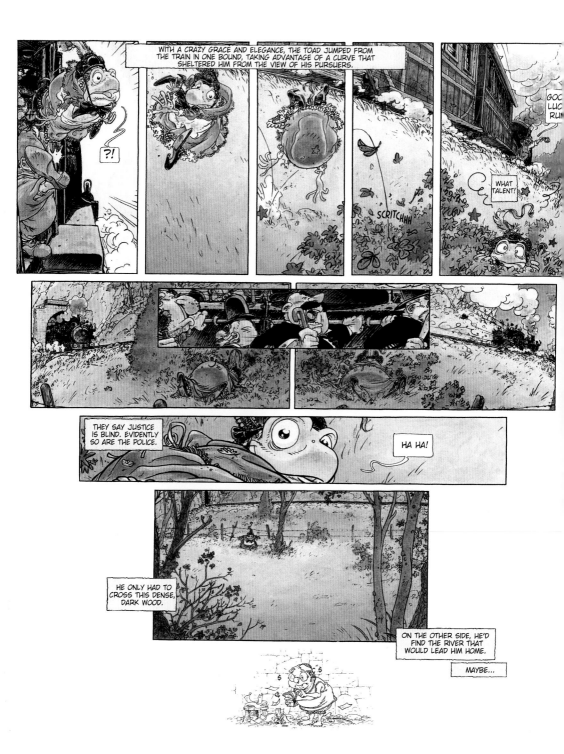

WITH A CRAZY GRACE AND ELEGANCE, THE TOAD JUMPED FROM THE TRAIN IN ONE BOUND, TAKING ADVANTAGE OF A CURVE THAT SHELTERED HIM FROM THE VIEW OF HIS PURSUERS.

?!

SCRITCHHH

GOC
LUC
RUI

WHAT TALENT!

THEY SAY JUSTICE IS BLIND. EVIDENTLY SO ARE THE POLICE.

HA HA!

HE ONLY HAD TO CROSS THIS DENSE, DARK WOOD.

ON THE OTHER SIDE, HE'D FIND THE RIVER THAT WOULD LEAD HIM HOME.

MAYBE...

Chapter IX

The Further Adventures of Toad

THAT STUPID NIGHT-MARE...AND THEN THE COLD...AND THIS STIFFNESS...

BRR RRR

OUCH...

KRAK!

A NEW DAY TO ENDURE... HE FELT SO MISERABLE...

OWW

SUDDENLY IT ALL CAME BACK.

HIS INSANITY, HIS SENTENCING, HIS PRISON, HIS ESCAPE, HIS FLIGHT, HIS PURSUIT...EVERYTHING.

FREE.

JUST MENTIONING THIS ONE WORD WARMED HIM.

A NEW DAY WAS BEGINNING. HE FELT INVULNERABLE.

HE HAD THE WORLD ALL TO HIMSELF.

THERE WAS BUT ONE SHADOW ON THIS PICTURE. HE NEEDED TO HIDE. HIS FACE WOULD BE PLASTERED ALL OVER THE PLACE BY NOW.

AFTER ALL, AS HE THOUGHT ABOUT IT, THERE MUST BE SOME KIND OF GLORY IN IT...HE HAD TO PAY FOR THAT.

LOST IN THOUGHT CONCERNING HIS GROWING FAME AT POLICE STATIONS, THE TOAD PLODDED ON PATIENTLY UNTIL HE SOON REACHED A CANAL.

HE DECIDED TO FOLLOW IT. NORMALLY, IT SHOULD END UP AT THE RIVER. AT WORST, BY THE SEA. FROM THERE, HE COULD ALWAYS TAKE OFF AND CONQUER THE NEW WORLD.

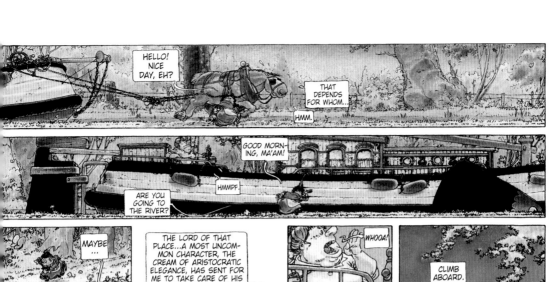

HELLO! NICE DAY, EH?

THAT DEPENDS FOR WHOM...

HMM.

GOOD MORNING, MA'AM!

HMMPF.

ARE YOU GOING TO THE RIVER?

MAYBE...

NEAR TOAD HALL?

HAVE TO SEE...

THE LORD OF THAT PLACE...A MOST UNCOMMON CHARACTER, THE CREAM OF ARISTOCRATIC ELEGANCE, HAS SENT FOR ME TO TAKE CARE OF HIS WASHING OF A RATHER GREAT VALUE...

CAN YOU TAKE ME THERE?

HUH?

WHOOA!

CLIMB ABOARD.

IF YOU WANT, I CAN HELP YOU STEER.

THE WORK'S TOO DIFFICULT FOR A DELICATE THING LIKE YOU.

SO, YOU'RE IN THE WASHING BUSINESS, MA'AM?

BEST IN THE WHOLE COUNTY! AH, WASHING! IRONING! BOILING! BLEACHING! IT'S MY LIFE!

MY JOY!

I HAVE AT LEAST 26 EMPLOYEES. OR 35. I DON'T KNOW ANYMORE...

I'M ALL ALONE. MY HUSBAND LEFT WITH THE DOG. "GONE SHOPPING," HE SAID. BUT I KNOW HIM! HE'S A LAZYBONES, HE IS.

AND HIS DOG'S EVEN WORSE!

SO, I WAS TELLING MYSELF, WE WOMEN HAVE TO HELP EACH OTHER...ANYWAY, WITH YOU, IT'S NOT REALLY A BURDEN...COME INTO THE CABIN WITH ME...

THE TOAD DIDN'T LIKE THE TURN IN THE CONVERSATION.

?!!

....!

THERE NOW. HAVE FUN!

89.

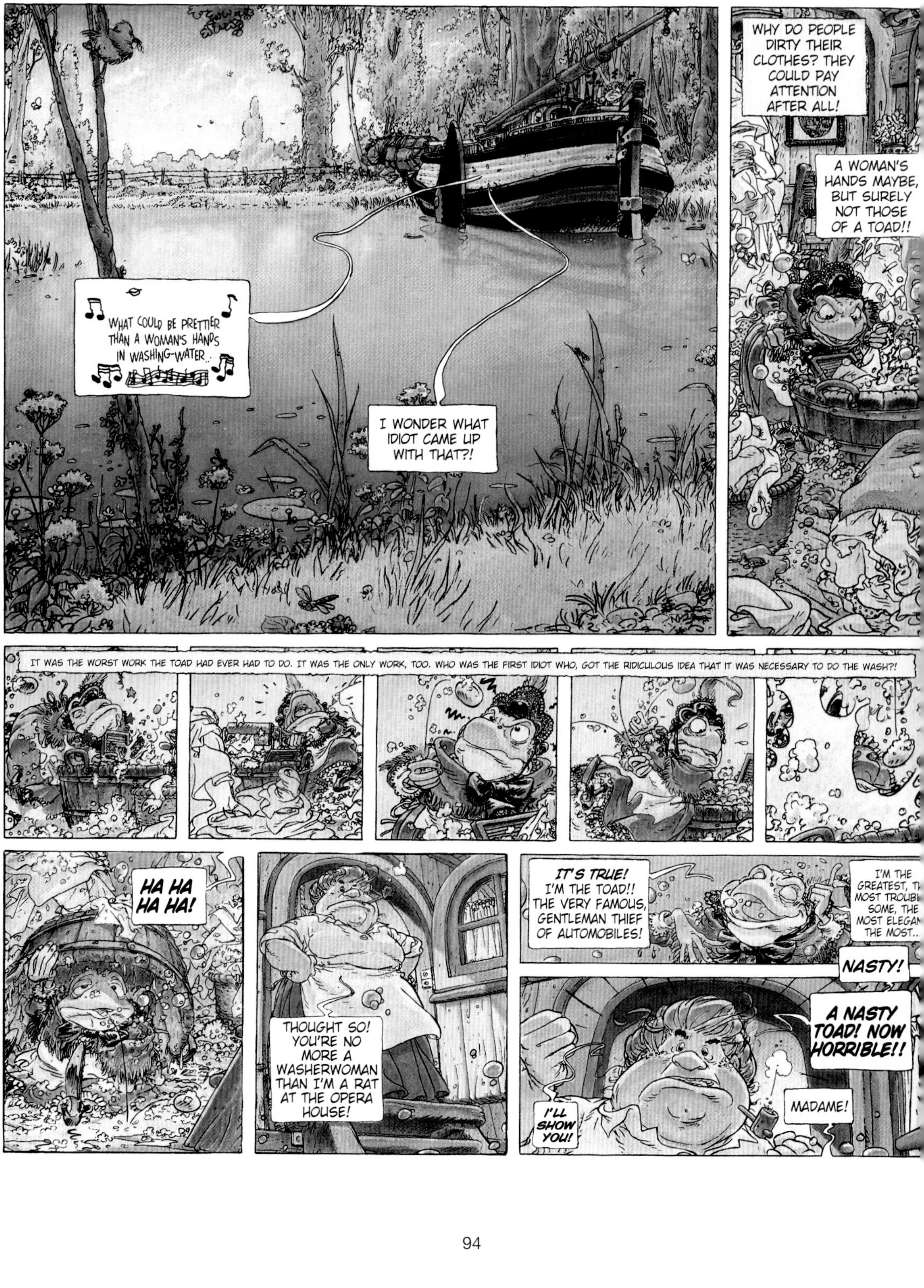
WHAT COULD BE PRETTIER THAN A WOMAN'S HANDS IN WASHING-WATER...
I WONDER WHAT IDIOT CAME UP WITH THAT?!
WHY DO PEOPLE DIRTY THEIR CLOTHES? THEY COULD PAY ATTENTION AFTER ALL!
A WOMAN'S HANDS MAYBE, BUT SURELY NOT THOSE OF A TOAD!!
IT WAS THE WORST WORK THE TOAD HAD EVER HAD TO DO. IT WAS THE ONLY WORK, TOO. WHO WAS THE FIRST IDIOT WHO, GOT THE RIDICULOUS IDEA THAT IT WAS NECESSARY TO DO THE WASH?!
HA HA HA HA!
THOUGHT SO! YOU'RE NO MORE A WASHERWOMAN THAN I'M A RAT AT THE OPERA HOUSE!
IT'S TRUE! I'M THE TOAD!! THE VERY FAMOUS, GENTLEMAN THIEF OF AUTOMOBILES!
I'M THE GREATEST, TH MOST TROUBL SOME, THE MOST ELEGAN THE MOST...
NASTY!
A NASTY TOAD! NOW HORRIBLE!!
I'LL SHOW YOU!
MADAME!

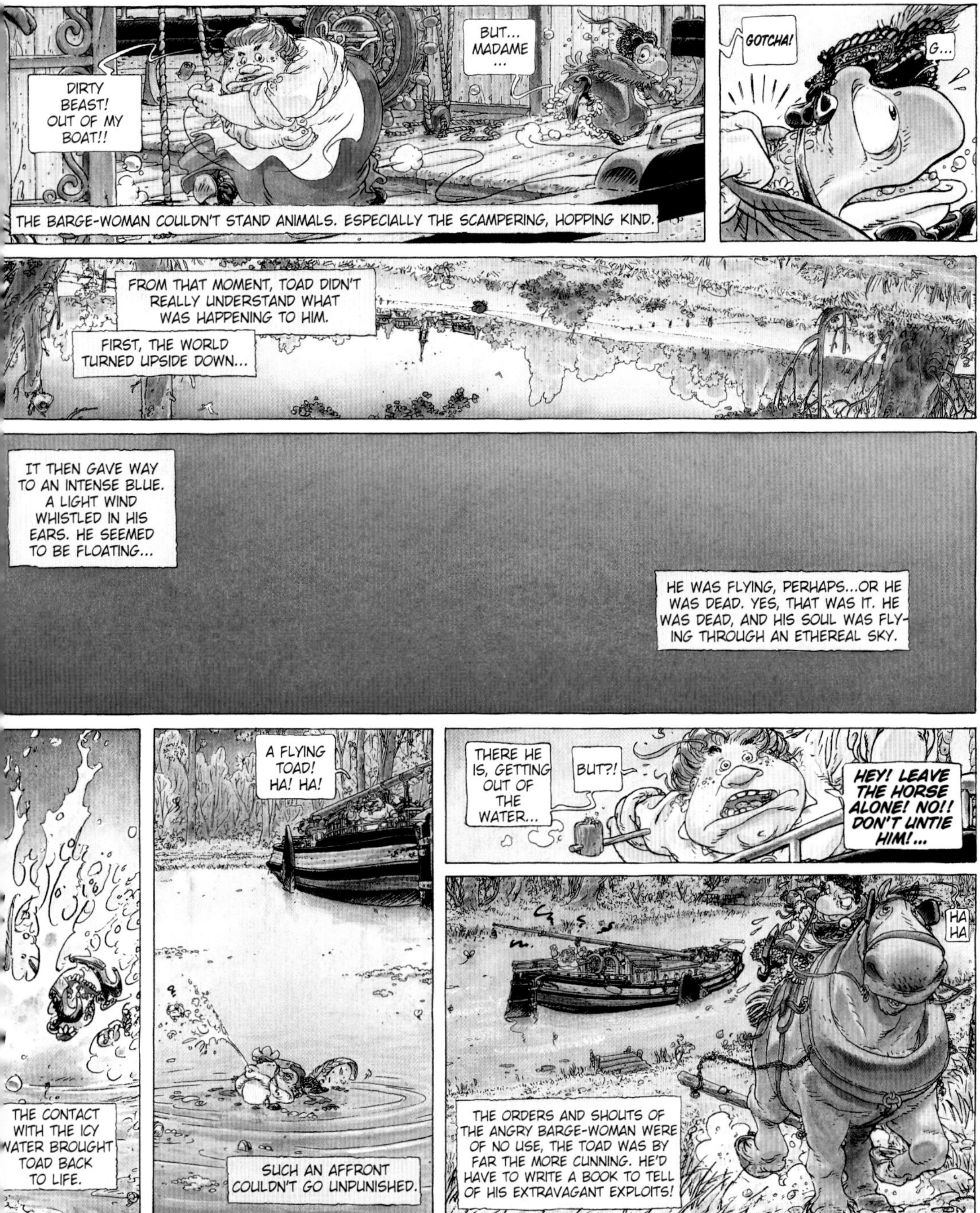
DIRTY BEAST! OUT OF MY BOAT!!
BUT... MADAME ...
THE BARGE-WOMAN COULDN'T STAND ANIMALS. ESPECIALLY THE SCAMPERING, HOPPING KIND.
GOTCHA!
G...
FROM THAT MOMENT, TOAD DIDN'T REALLY UNDERSTAND WHAT WAS HAPPENING TO HIM.
FIRST, THE WORLD TURNED UPSIDE DOWN...
IT THEN GAVE WAY TO AN INTENSE BLUE. A LIGHT WIND WHISTLED IN HIS EARS. HE SEEMED TO BE FLOATING...
HE WAS FLYING, PERHAPS...OR HE WAS DEAD. YES, THAT WAS IT. HE WAS DEAD, AND HIS SOUL WAS FLYING THROUGH AN ETHEREAL SKY.
THE CONTACT WITH THE ICY WATER BROUGHT TOAD BACK TO LIFE.
A FLYING TOAD! HA! HA!
SUCH AN AFFRONT COULDN'T GO UNPUNISHED.
THERE HE IS, GETTING OUT OF THE WATER...
BUT?!
HEY! LEAVE THE HORSE ALONE! NO!! DON'T UNTIE HIM!...
HA HA
THE ORDERS AND SHOUTS OF THE ANGRY BARGE-WOMAN WERE OF NO USE, THE TOAD WAS BY FAR THE MORE CUNNING. HE'D HAVE TO WRITE A BOOK TO TELL OF HIS EXTRAVAGANT EXPLOITS!

PERCHED ON HIS PROUD STEED, HE WAS READY TO BATTLE AN ENTIRE ARMY, BUT THE HORSE'S RHYTHMIC TROT WASN'T VERY STIMULATING AND SOON, TOAD, OVERWHELMED WITH EMOTIONS, FELL ASLEEP.

SNOOOOORE

FRRRR

WAKING UP, HE FOUND HIMSELF ON A GORSE-DOTTED HEATH SWEPT BY THE WINDS.

STEW!

IT SMELLED LIKE STEW!

SNIF?

HE DIDN'T TAKE LONG IN DISCOVERING ITS ORIGIN.

HELLO! NICE WEATHER FOR THE SEASON, EH?

LO

THAT LOOKS AWFULLY GOOD!

HARD TO RESIST...

TCHAC!

GLOOPS

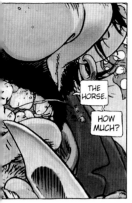

THE HORSE.

HOW MUCH?

UH..THIS IS A HORSE OF GREAT VALUE. HE'S A BLOOD HORSE, PARTLY, AND I...

3 SHILLINGS.

3 SHILLINGS?!!

...AND THE RIGHT TO EAT MY FILL OF THIS FRAGRANT, APPETIZING DISH.

IT'S A DEAL!

GLOOP
GLOOP
GLOOP
GLOOP
GLOOP

3 SHILLINGS... SOLD ME FOR 3 SHILLINGS... HOW SHAMEFUL.

GLUTTED AND CONVINCED HE HAD GLORIOUSLY MADE THE DEAL OF THE CENTURY, TOAD GOT UNDERWAY AGAIN.

THE WORLD HAS HELD GREAT HEROES, AS HISTORY-BOOKS HAVE SHOWED, BUT NEVER A NAME TO GO DOWN TO FAME COMPARED WITH THAT OF TOAD! THE CLEVER MEN AT OXFORD KNOW ALL THAT THERE IS TO BE KNOWED, BUT THEY NONE OF THEM KNOW ONE HALF AS MUCH AS INTELLIGENT MR. TOAD!

SUDDENLY, AROUND A CURVE IN THE ROAD...

THE FAMILIAR POOP-POOP OF AN AUTOMOBILE?...

POOP
POOP
POOP POOP

!

ONLY TOO WELL KNOWN!

IT WAS THE VERY ONE HE HAD STOLEN!!

TOO LATE...

OH, AR!

A LITTLE OLD LADY...JUST LIKE UR MOTHER...

CAN WE GIVE YOU A LIFT SOMEWHERE, MA'AM?

OOFH!

SCREECH

UH...INDEED, BUT COULD YOU LET ME DRIVE? I'M ALWAYS AFRAID WHEN I DON'T DRIVE...

PLEASE...

IT CERTAINLY IS THE DAY FOR HITCHHIKING!

OH OOH...

WE JUST PICKED UP THIS BARGE-MAN AND HIS DOG...

OH?

BE CAREFUL, THE CLUTCH IS FRAGILE.

93.

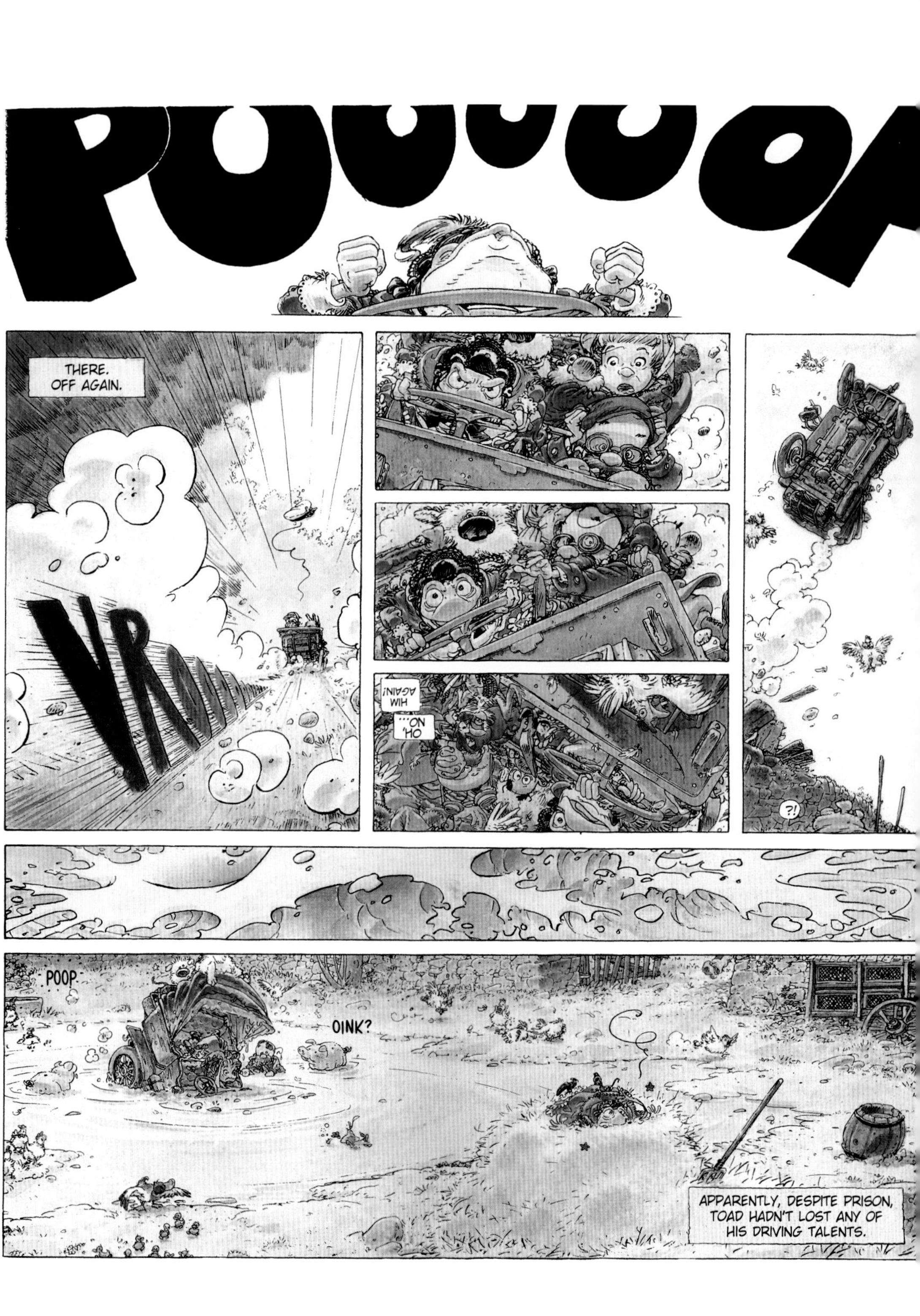
POOOOOP
THERE. OFF AGAIN.
VROOO
OH, NO... HIM AGAIN!
?!
POOP
OINK?
APPARENTLY, DESPITE PRISON, TOAD HADN'T LOST ANY OF HIS DRIVING TALENTS.

HAHA! LOOK! IT'S ME, HE TOAD!! THE ANIMAL ESCAPE ARTIST!

I GOT YOU, YOU SUCKERS!

TOAD!!

HIM AGAIN?!

MY CAR!

WHAT HAPPENED HERE?

OINK

LUCKILY, TOAD WAS THE BEST RUNNER IN THE WORLD. HE WAS EASILY GOING TO OUTRUN THEM, TO MAKE FUN OF THEM, TOO...

HE DIDN'T SEE THE EDGE OF THE BANK.

THE BELLY FLOP HE DID WHEN HE HIT THE WATER KNOCKED HIM OUT. HE STILL STRUGGLED A LITTLE AGAINST THE CURRENT PULLING HIM.

THEN HE SANK.

IT REALLY SEEMED THAT, THIS TIME, THE WORLD WAS RID OF TOAD.

FOR GOOD.

SOMETHING PRICKED HIS BACKSIDE...

Chapter X

"Like Summer Tempests Came His Tears

IT'S NOT TRUE! I AIN'T LITTLE! YOU'RE SAYING THAT 'CAUSE YOU JUST DON'T KNOW HOW!!

YEAH, I DO. FIRST...

...YOU HAVE TO SMELL THE AIR, OBSERVE THE LIGHT, TASTE THE WATER, FEEL THE CURRENT, YOU HAVE TO...HAVE TO...

HMM...

...YOU HAVE TO THINK "FISH"!

THINK FISH?!!

YES, ONLY THEN WILL YOU KNOW WHERE TO LOOK FOR HIM.

HA HA HA! "THINK FISH"! BLUB BLUB HA HA!

SILLY FOOL! WHAT DID YOU THINK FISHING WAS? JUST TOSSING YOUR BAIT IN WHEREVER...

...AND EXPECTING A FISH TO SWIM BY...

?!!

WELL, WHAT ALREADY?! WE CAN'T JUST SIT HERE, CAN WE?!!!?

CALM DOWN, OTTER.

THE LAWYER TOLD YOU WE COULDN'T DO ANYTHING ELSE FOR TOAD, EXCEPT PERHAPS REQUESTING THAT HE BE TRANSFERRED TO AN INSANE ASYLUM.

FRANKLY, I DON'T KNOW IF THAT'S BETTER THAN PRISON.

I GOT AN IDEA!

WE BUST IN AND TAKE ON THE LOT OF 'EM!

FORGET IT, THERE ARE TOO MANY HUMANS. AND THE LAW'S THE LAW, TOO. HE'S MADE A MISTAKE AND MUST PAY.

YOU'RE PROBABLY RIGHT.

STILL, I'LL MISS HIM.

?

UHH...EXCUSE ME, BUT MY BROTHER AND I JUST FISHED UP SOMETHING STRANGE.

BIZARRE, EVEN.

!

A SEA MONSTER?!

WITH PINK FEATH- ERS?!!

YES. AND HUUUUUGE! MY BROTHER WANTED TO THINK FISH, BUT HE SHOULD HAVE BEEN THINKING FEATHER-MONSTER.

?!!

"THINK FISH"?...

THERE! YOU SEE?

?

?

WHY..IT'S NOT A MONSTER... YOU'D ALMOST SAY IT WAS A HALF-DROWNED WASHERWOMAN...

EH?

UGGHH...

A WASHER- WOMAN?

LET ME DO IT!

SAY, DON'T YOU HAVE SCHOOL TODAY?

SOME HAVE SAID I'M A MASTER IN THE ART OF MOUTH- TO-MOUTH.

UHH...

IT'S...IT'S FOR OUR FIELD WORK IN NATURAL SCIENCES, SIR...

HHHMFFF...

MMMH

PFFFFFFFFFF

UHH...

SORRY, GUYS...

I'V DON ALL CAN

SO MUCH UNHAPPINESS... TOAD...THIS WASHER- WOMAN NOW...WHY? WHY DO WE ALWAYS HAVE TO BE POWERLESS FACING THE RELENTLESSNESS OF FATE?...WHY?

WHEW... MY HEAD'S SPIN- NING A LITTLE.

WELL, 'CAUSE THAT'S HOW IT IS?

GARGLLUB

KOF KOF

OOPS! SORRY...

SPLIT!

WHO'S THE IMPUDENT RAS- CAL WHO DARES SIT HIS CRUDE BOTTOM ON THE MOST DELICATE OF POTBELLIES?

HIM?!

YUCK! THAT'S WHAT I KISSED? BLEAH! BLEAH! BLEAH!

102

IT WOULD HAVE TAKEN US SOME TWENTY EXTRA PAGES TO GIVE A GOOD ACCOUNTING OF THE REUNION WITH TOAD - FOR IT WAS HE. SO LET'S JOIN OUR FRIENDS AT THE RAT'S HOME.

HEY, ISN'T YOUR SCHOOL THAT WAY?

THAT REALLY IS TOAD! WE'RE FRETTING AND HE'S OFF FROLICKING IN THE RIVER DRESSED FOR CARNIVAL!

SUFFICE IT TO SAY THAT RAT WAS SO HAPPY THAT HE FELT ALMOST CAPABLE OF FORGIVING HIM FOR HIS BLUNDERS, WHIMS, AND ALL THOSE LITTLE FAULTS THAT MAKE TOAD TOAD...

?!!

MY WAXED FLOOR!

MY ORIENTAL RUG!

GO OFF UPSTAIRS AT ONCE, CLEAN YOURSELF AND CHANGE CLOTHES! AND SCRUB WELL BEHIND YOUR EARS!

AND PUT ON SOME SLIPPERS!

...HMM, ALMOST...

TOAD DID AS RAT TOLD HIM.

ALTHOUGH HE DIDN'T UNDERSTAND WHAT USE SLIPPERS WERE WHILE WASHING...

AHHH...THE PLEASURE IN FORGETTING ONESELF UNDER THAT FINE, HOT SHOWER...TO LET HIS PROBLEMS AND ACCUMULATED ERRORS DRAIN AWAY WITH THE DIRT AND MUD...

HMM...

AND SOON, WASHED, BRUSHED, DRESSED UP, AND PERFUMED, THE NEW TOAD MADE HIS APPEARANCE.

TA-DA!

YOU COULD REALLY TELL: HE NOW FELT LIKE A NEW ANIMAL.

COME HAVE SOMETHING TO EAT WHILE TELLING US OF YOUR ADVENTURES. I'M GUESSING YOU MUST HAVE GOOD STORIES FULL OF BRAWLS!

WE'VE MADE A SNACK FOR YOU LIKE YOU HAVEN'T HAD FOR A LONG TIME.

LOTS OF GOOD THINGS: BERGAMOT TEA, BAKED APPLES, COPIOUSLY BUTTERED TOAST AND MUFFINS...

SORRY, I DON'T HAVE ANY MORE ORANGE MARMALADE.

AND TOAD SET TO EATING, EATING, EATING; TO TALKING, TALKING, TALKING; TO SPLUTTERING, TOO. AND ESPECIALLY TO BOASTING.

YESH, YESH, I ASSURE YOU! A HORDE OF A HUNDRED-FIFTY FURIOUSH SHAILORS!

NOOOO...

IT'S INCREDI-BLE...

ISN'T IT?

HUMPH!

WHAT'S INCREDIBLE IS THAT NONE OF YOUR MISADVENTURES HAS TAUGHT YOU A LESSON! WHAT A BRAGGART YOU ARE! I'M SURE THAT AT THE FIRST BACKFIRE, YOU'LL START AGAIN...

THINK OF YOUR FRIENDS! I DON'T WANT YOU TO GO BACK TO PRISON!

DO YOU THINK IT'S ANY PLEASURE FOR ME TO HEAR IT SAID THAT I'M THE CHAP THAT KEEPS COMPANY WITH JAILBIRDS?!!

WELL...

GULP.

AS ALWAYS, YOU'RE RIGHT. NO MORE CARS AND INOPPORTUNE DRIVING...

THE FACT IS, JUST NOW, WHILE I WAS DROWNING, I HAD A SUDDEN IDEA CONNECTED WITH MOTORBOATS AND...

I GOT IT! HE WAS THINKING FISH!!

OKAY. YOU'RE QUITE RIGHT. FROM NOW ON, I'LL BE GOOD AND PEACEFUL AND WORRY ABOUT MY ROSES, KEEP A PONY-CHAISE AND ALL THOSE THINGS THAT MAKE UP THE LIFE OF A GENTLEMAN OF PROPERTY...

IT'LL BE WONDERFUL...

YIPPE

WHAT?! YOU HAVEN'T HEARD?!!

HEARD WHAT? YOU'RE STARTING TO WORRY ME.

YOU SHOULD!

HERE. READ THIS.

...

ALL THE SLIGHTEST DETAILS HAVE BEEN SET DOWN THERE.

DO YOU REMEMBER MOLE'S NOTEPADS? WHERE HE JOTS DOWN AND DRAWS EVERYTHING THAT HAPPENS TO HIM...

WHAT TOAD DISCOVERED IN THEM WAS QUITE SIMPLY CATASTROPHIC.

The 3rd Toad's incarceration. After thought we'd hit rock bottom. But things were going to get even worse yet. As soon as they learned of our unfortunate friends' guilty verdict, the waterfowl quick-ly spread the news throughout the land. The weasels from the old Wild Wood and their usual partners-in-crime, the ferrets and stoats, always up to no good, started say-ing it was wasteful to leave such a large house unoccu-pied in such miserable times and that it was necessary to lodge the neediest in Toad Hall. We were rather non-plussed: what could we say in opposition to such a generous idea.

But when it really got bad is when they said that they were the needy! So we immediately took the neces-sary measures. Badger and I moved to the manor and kept guard whereas Rat attended to both the house-keeping and the affairs of our wretch, meaning our friend. The Otter, to his great regret, can scarcely leave his home, for he must watch his children while his wife visits a sick relative. As for the field mice and the other small animals–not for getting the rabbits–they are too afraid of those dreadful adversaries. We're not...

CRAC

AS HE WENT ALONG IN HIS READING, THE TOAD PER-SUADED HIMSELF THAT SOME TERRIBLE, IRREPARABLE, NO DOUBT IRREVERSIBLE THING WAS GOING TO OCCUR. HE THEN FELT HIS TEARS IRREPRESSIBLY RISING WITHIN HIMSELF...

DID YOU SEE THE LITTLE DRAWINGS?

FUNNY, NO?

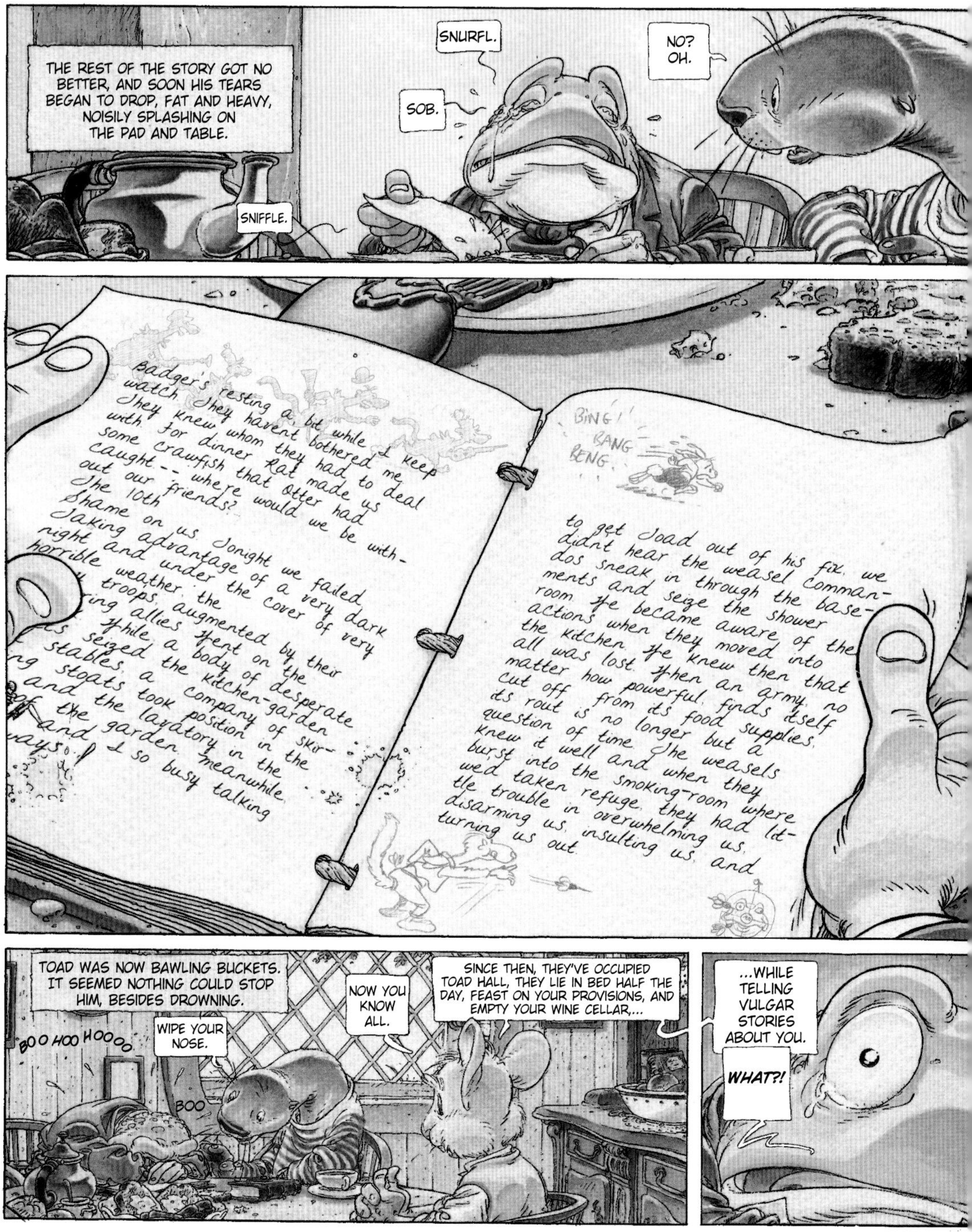
THE REST OF THE STORY GOT NO BETTER, AND SOON HIS TEARS BEGAN TO DROP, FAT AND HEAVY, NOISILY SPLASHING ON THE PAD AND TABLE.
SNURFL.
SOB.
SNIFFLE.
NO? OH.
Badger's resting a bit while I keep
watch. They haven't bothered me.
They knew whom they had to deal
with. For dinner Rat made us
some crawfish that Otter had
caught -- where would we be without our friends?
The 10th
Shame on us. Tonight we failed.
Taking advantage of a very dark
night and under the cover of very
horrible weather, the
troops, augmented by their
ing allies spent on the
While a body of desperate
seized the kitchen-garden
stables, a company of skir-
stoats took position in the
and the lavatory in the
the garden. Meanwhile,
and I so busy talking
to get Toad out of his fix, we
didn't hear the weasel comman-
dos sneak in through the base-
ments and seize the shower
room. We became aware of the
actions when they moved into
the kitchen. We knew then that
all was lost. When an army, no
matter how powerful, finds itself
cut off from its food supplies,
its rout is no longer but a
question of time. The weasels
knew it well and when they
burst into the smoking-room where
we'd taken refuge, they had little trouble in overwhelming us,
disarming us, insulting us, and
turning us out.
BING! BANG BENG.
TOAD WAS NOW BAWLING BUCKETS. IT SEEMED NOTHING COULD STOP HIM, BESIDES DROWNING.
BOO HOO HOOOO
WIPE YOUR NOSE.
BOO
NOW YOU KNOW ALL.
SINCE THEN, THEY'VE OCCUPIED TOAD HALL, THEY LIE IN BED HALF THE DAY, FEAST ON YOUR PROVISIONS, AND EMPTY YOUR WINE CELLAR,...
...WHILE TELLING VULGAR STORIES ABOUT YOU.
WHAT?!

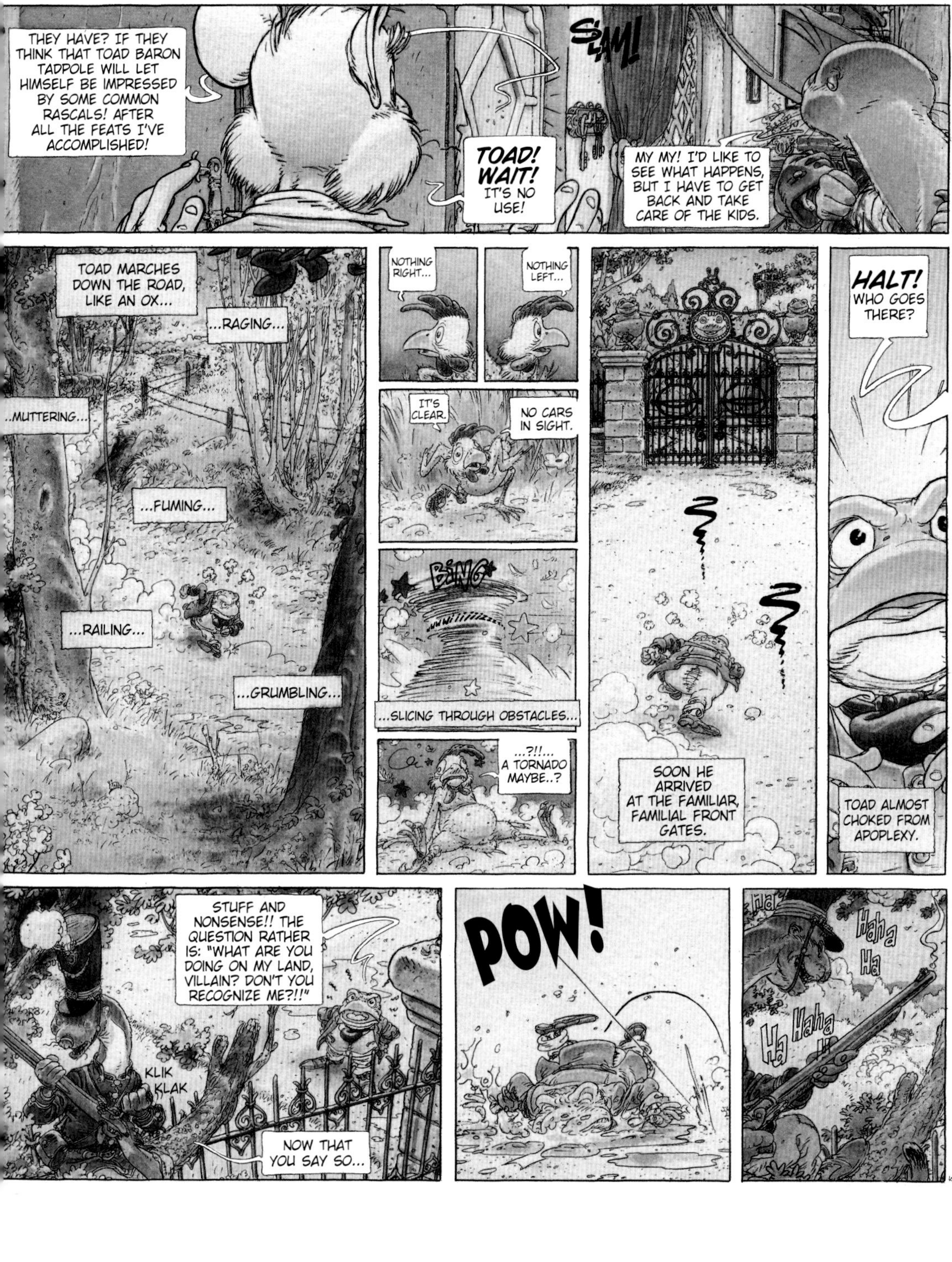
THEY HAVE? IF THEY THINK THAT TOAD BARON TADPOLE WILL LET HIMSELF BE IMPRESSED BY SOME COMMON RASCALS! AFTER ALL THE FEATS I'VE ACCOMPLISHED!
SLAM!
TOAD! WAIT! IT'S NO USE!
MY MY! I'D LIKE TO SEE WHAT HAPPENS, BUT I HAVE TO GET BACK AND TAKE CARE OF THE KIDS.
TOAD MARCHES DOWN THE ROAD, LIKE AN OX...
...RAGING...
...MUTTERING...
...FUMING...
...RAILING...
...GRUMBLING...
NOTHING RIGHT...
NOTHING LEFT...
IT'S CLEAR.
NO CARS IN SIGHT.
BING
...SLICING THROUGH OBSTACLES...
...?!!... A TORNADO MAYBE..?
SOON HE ARRIVED AT THE FAMILIAR, FAMILIAL FRONT GATES.
HALT! WHO GOES THERE?
TOAD ALMOST CHOKED FROM APOPLEXY.
STUFF AND NONSENSE!! THE QUESTION RATHER IS: "WHAT ARE YOU DOING ON MY LAND, VILLAIN? DON'T YOU RECOGNIZE ME?!!"
KLIK KLAK
NOW THAT YOU SAY SO...
POW!
Haha Ha
Ha Haha

SO? HOW DID IT GO?

BAD.

OFF ALREADY?

AFTER CHANGING IN A FLASH, OR ALMOST, TOAD ROWED UP THE RIVER TO THE EDGES OF HIS DOMAIN.

HIS DEAR MANOR HOUSE...

IT WAS STILL THERE, TRANQUIL AND KINDLY, CROWNED WITH WHITE PIGEONS. THE GARDENS BLAZED IN THE EVENING SUNSHINE. ALL TRANQUIL AND AWAITING HIS RETURN...

HE WOULD TRY THE BOAT-HOUSE FIRST...

EVERY-THING WAS GOING WELL UNTIL...

!?!

KRAAK

SPLASH

LOOK! A PADDLING, PRISONER, TAD-POLE!

HEEEE

TEE HEE TEE HEE

HA HA

HO HO

PUDDLE-ING! HAHAHA HAHA!

HO HO! SURE IS A WET ONE TODAY, BOYS...THE FROG'S FLOUNDERING IN HIS FISH BOWL!! HAHA!

YUCK YUCK

IT WILL BE YOUR HEAD NEXT TIME, TOADY!

HA HA

TEEE HEEE HEEE

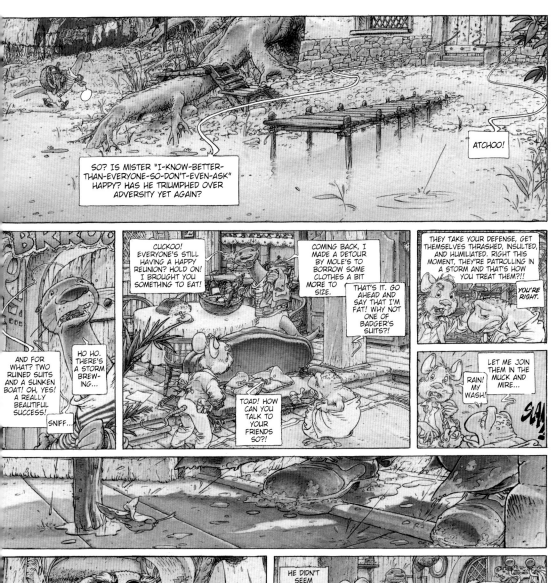

SO? IS MISTER "I-KNOW-BETTER-THAN-EVERYONE-SO-DON'T-EVEN-ASK" HAPPY? HAS HE TRIUMPHED OVER ADVERSITY YET AGAIN?

ATCHOO!

CUCKOO! EVERYONE'S STILL HAVING A HAPPY REUNION? HOLD ON! I BROUGHT YOU SOMETHING TO EAT!

COMING BACK, I MADE A DETOUR BY MOLE'S TO BORROW SOME CLOTHES A BIT MORE TO SIZE.

THAT'S IT. GO AHEAD AND SAY THAT I'M FAT! WHY NOT ONE OF BADGER'S SUITS?!

THEY TAKE YOUR DEFENSE, GET THEMSELVES THRASHED, INSULTED, AND HUMILIATED. RIGHT THIS MOMENT, THEY'RE PATROLLING IN A STORM AND THAT'S HOW YOU TREAT THEM?!!

YOU'RE RIGHT.

AND FOR WHAT? TWO RUINED SUITS AND A SUNKEN BOAT! OH, YES! A REALLY BEAUTIFUL SUCCESS!

SNIFF...

HO HO. THERE'S A STORM BREWING...

TOAD! HOW CAN YOU TALK TO YOUR FRIENDS SO?!

RAIN! MY WASH!

LET ME JOIN THEM IN THE MUCK AND MIRE...

SLAM!

...IT WAS BADGER.

HE DIDN'T SEEM SURPRISED AT TOAD'S PRESENCE AND GREETED HIM LIKE SOMEONE OFFERING CONDO-LENCES...

OH, UNHAPPY TOAD!

THEN HE WENT TO EAT.

NEVER MIND, HE'S ALWAYS RATHER LOW WHEN HIS STOMACH IS EMPTY...

OH?

GOOD HEAVENS! WHAT WEATHER!

?

SLAM

TOAD SADLY SAW HIS MEAL FAST DISAPPEARING...

TOAD! HOW HAPPY I AM TO SEE YOU! THEY FINALLY SET YOU FREE?

UHH...NOT REALLY...

I MADE A LITTLE ESCAPE...

I CAPTURED A RAILWAY TRAIN, FLOUTED THE CONSTABULARY, I GOT INTO INTERNATIONAL COMMERCE FOR A TIME, BUT SOME SAY THAT'S NOTHING...

I'M FAMISHED. SUPPOSING YOU TALK WHILE I EAT.

I THINK IT WOULD BE BEST IF YOU TELL US WHAT THE POSITION IS...

OH, MY! THE POSITION'S ABOUT AS BAD AS IT CAN BE. THERE ARE WEASELS, FERRETS, AND STOATS EVERYWHERE. THEY FIRE AT YOU AND MOCK YOU.

CRUNCH

GULP.

HOW THEY DO LAUGH! THAT'S WHAT ANNOYS ME MOST.

HMM, I SEE. WHAT TOAD REALLY OUGHT TO DO...

NO!

NO, HE OUGHTN'T! YOU DON'T UNDERSTAND. WHAT HE OUGHT TO DO IS, HE OUGHT TO—

WELL, I SHAN'T DO IT, ANYWAY! I'M NOT GOING TO BE ORDERED ABOUT BY YOU FELLOWS! NO! WHAT I'M GOING TO DO......IS BUST IN THERE AND SMACK 'EM AROUND!

HMM...

?

QUIET!

IT'S TIME TO GET TO BED, ROSEMARY AND RED! TOMORROW WE'LL ALL BE CALMER.

...BUT... I'VE NOT YET EATEN...

OH! SORRY ...

WHEN BADGER USED THAT TONE OF VOICE, THEY ALL KNEW THEY'D BEST LISTEN.

BAH! THERE'S PLENTY LEFT TO SATISFY TOAD! HE JUST NOW TOLD US THAT WAS HIS DAILY FARE AND THAT HE WAS QUITE HAPPY WITH IT.

UHH ...

THE NEXT DAY, STILL GROGGY WITH THE FLEETING FRAGMENTS OF HIS TRIUMPHANT DREAMS, TOAD CAME DOWN LATE IN THE MORNING, AS USUAL. OTTER WAS SORRY, BUT HE'D HAD TO RETURN HOME. MOLE HAD SLIPPED OFF EARLY, WITHOUT TELLING ANYONE WHERE HE WAS GOING.

ZZ.

RAT WAS RUNNING AROUND THE ROOM, ASSEMBLING WEAPONS FOR EVENTUAL ACTION. AS FOR BADGER, HE WAS MEDITATING, HIS HANDKERCHIEF OVER HIS NOSE.

SLAM!

I'VE GOT NEWS, MY FRIENDS!

?!!

THIS MORNING, I GOT AN IDEA WHEN I SAW THIS OLD DRESS. I PUT IT ON AND OFF I WENT TO TOAD HALL TO OFFER MY SERVICES.

?!!

THEY GAVE ME THEIR BOXERS TO WASH AND, OF COURSE, THEY GAVE ME A HARD TIME!

BUT I LEARNED THAT THEY'RE GIVING A BANQUET TONIGHT IN HONOR OF A SOLICITOR'S ARRIVAL AND THE SIGNING OF SOME DOCUMENT.

HMM.

THE PROPERTY DEED! WE'RE DONE FOR?!

HAHH... DISGUISED AS A WASHERWOMAN... WHAT A RIDICULOUS IDEA!!

SO, I DON'T KNOW WHAT CAME OVER ME, BUT I TOLD THEM TO ENJOY IT, FOR TOMORROW AN ARMY OF RATS, BADGERS, TOADS, AND MOLES WILL HAVE CHASED THEM OFF.

HA! YOU SHOULDA SEEN 'EM!

ARE YOU MAD?!

ON THE CONTRARY, MOLE HAS MANAGED EXCELLENTLY.

?

WHEN WE ATTACK THE MANOR TONIGHT, THEY'LL BE SO UPSET, THEY'LL THINK THEY'RE BEING ATTACKED ON ALL SIDES AT ONCE.

WE STILL HAVE TO GET IN!

I'M GOING TO TELL YOU A GREAT SECRET.

107.

HMM.

YOUR FATHER, TOAD, WHO WAS A WORTHY ANIMAL - A LOT WORTHIER THAN SOME OTHERS I KNOW - DISCOVERED AN UNDERGROUND PASSAGE LEADING RIGHT INTO THE MIDDLE OF THE CASTLE. HE PATIENTLY REPAIRED IT, PROPPED IT UP, RENOVATED AND CLEANED IT OUT...

HE MADE ME SWEAR TO ONLY REVEAL ITS EXISTENCE TO YOU AS A LAST RESORT.

O, NONSENSE! BADGER. WHY DID PAPA NEVER MENTION IT TO ME? HE TOLD ME ALL KINDS OF SECRETS, THAT HIDING PLACE IN THE CHIMNEY, FOR EX...

UHH...

...OKAY, I GET IT.

PERHAPS I AM A BIT OF A TALKER. I HAVE A GIFT. I'VE BEEN TOLD I OUGHT TO HAVE A SALON.

...YOU KNOW HOW IT IS, MY FRIENDS GET ROUND ME, WE CHAFF, WE SPARKLE, WE TELL WITTY STORIES, AND SOMEHOW MY TONGUE GETS WAGGING, FOR FEAR THAT SOMEONE MIGHT JUMP IN, OR WORSE, THAT IT GETS QUIET...

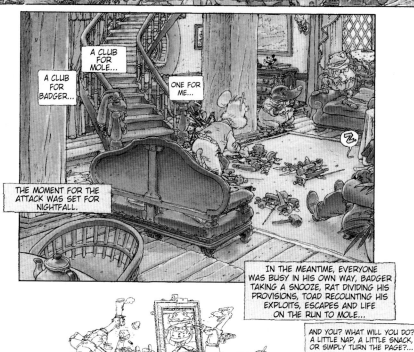

A CLUB FOR MOLE...

A CLUB FOR BADGER...

ONE FOR ME...

THE MOMENT FOR THE ATTACK WAS SET FOR NIGHTFALL.

IN THE MEANTIME, EVERYONE WAS BUSY IN HIS OWN WAY, BADGER TAKING A SNOOZE, RAT DIVIDING HIS PROVISIONS, TOAD RECOUNTING HIS EXPLOITS, ESCAPES AND LIFE ON THE RUN TO MOLE...

AND YOU? WHAT WILL YOU DO? A LITTLE NAP, A LITTLE SNACK, OR SIMPLY TURN THE PAGE?...

Chapter XI

The Return of Ulysses

CAREFUL, TOAD...

THE MOSS IS SLIPPERY, I KNOW. I'M NOT DEAF!

DON'T GET FAR BEHIND ME AND WATCH WHERE YOU PUT YOUR FEET.

SPLASH!

THEY SOON GOT UNDERWAY AGAIN. AT LAST THEY WERE IN THE SECRET PASSAGE.

THE EXPEDITION HAD REALLY BEGUN!

TOAD WAS SHIVERING. HE HEARD HIS TEETH CLATTERING IN A DIABOLIC RHYTHM. WAS IT THE COLD? WAS IT DREAD?

HE WAS WET THROUGH AND THE COLD AIR WAS CHILLING HIS WET CLOTHES.

EVEN WORSE, HE FEARED THE DARK. EVER SINCE THAT DAY WHEN, TO PUNISH HIM FOR SETTING THE STABLES ON FIRE WITH HIS SHADOW THEATRE, HIS FATHER HAD SHUT HIM IN THE BASEMENT FOR TEN MINUTES.

HE SPENT THEM HIDING UNDER AN OLD COVER, TRYING TO CONCEAL HIMSELF FROM THE MONSTERS OF THE DARK, GIANT ROACHES, AND CANNIBAL SPIDERS THAT SURELY LIVED THERE.

HA!

LOST IN THOUGHT, TOAD ALLOWED HIMSELF TO FALL BEHIND...

AAAHH

TOAD BOLTED SO QUICKLY, THE OTHERS, BECAUSE OF THE DARKNESS, DIDN'T SEE HIM COMING AND THOUGHT THEY WERE BEING ATTACKED FROM BEHIND.

OOPS!

POM

HA!

AN ATTACK FROM THE REAR! GET DOWN, I'LL COVER YOU!!

?!!

?

AND FOR A MOMENT ALL WAS CONFUSION...

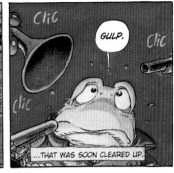

Clic

Clic

Clic

GULP.

...THAT WAS SOON CLEARED UP.

NOW THIS TIME THAT TIRESOME TOAD SHALL BE LEFT BEHIND!

TOAD WILL STAY HERE AND NOT BUDGE UNTIL WE'VE FINISHED AND COME BACK FOR HIM!!

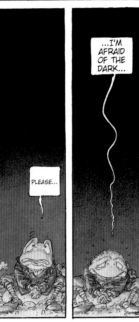

PLEASE...

...I'M AFRAID OF THE DARK...

EVEN IF HE'D NOT BEEN THEIR FRIEND, THEY STILL COULDN'T HAVE ABANDONED HIM...

IT WAS THE ONLY ANIMAL THING TO DO.

IT SEEMED THAT THEY WERE FINALLY ARRIVING AT THEIR DESTINATION.

IT'S LIKE THERE'S SOMETHING BLOCKING IT.

PUSH!

BOOM!

DARN!

SHHH...

THE NOISE, AS THEY EMERGED FROM THE PASSAGE, WAS SIMPLY DEAFENING. ACCLAMATIONS, DECLAMATIONS, FISTS POUNDING ON THE TABLES. THE PARTY WAS GOING FULL TILT.

NGH!

IT'S OKAY. THEY DIDN'T HEAR ANYTHING.

I DON'T SEE ANYONE.

I'LL OPEN.

NO! CAREFUL!

HA! HA! THE CHIEF! WHAT AN ORATOR!

OH, YEA HA HA! WHAT A SPEECH! CAN STIL HEAR IT

"MY DEAR BRETHREN, MY DEAR ACCOMPLICES, REST ASSURED, THIS SPEECH WILL BE BRIEF...

...BUT BEFORE I RESUME MY SEAT...

(GREAT APPLAUSE)

(RENEWED CHEERING)

HEH!

ALL THIS FOOD...

THEY HAD TO RESIST DESPITE THE HUNGER TORMENTING THEM. THE SLIGHTEST SOUND RISKED BETRAYING THEM.

...I SHOULD LIKE TO SAY ONE WORD ABOUT OUR KIND HOST, MR. TOAD.

WE ALL KNOW TOAD!

(GREAT LAUGHTER)

HA!

WH...

OW...

"GOOD TOAD, MODEST TOAD, HONEST TOAD!

WHO SO KINDLY LEFT HIS DOMAIN TO US, PREFERRING TO IT, THE JOYS OF MEDITATIVE CONFINEMENT."

(SHRIEKS OF MERRIMENT)

HO HO!

GARGLE!

HOHO. I'M STILL HUNGRY... I'M GOING TO GET A TIN OF GOOSE LIVER FROM THE PANTRY. IT TASTES FUNNY, BUT WITH PICKLES AND MAYONNAISE, YOU CAN EAT IT...

HEE HEE HEE

WAN SOM

GUULK!

MY GOOSE LIVER!

THE PANTRY? OH, MY, OH,

WAIT!...AND WHEN HE STARTED THE SONG!

HOHO! HOW DID IT GO, OH, YEAH...

PHEW!...

"TOAD HE WENT A-PLEASURING GAILY DOWN THE STREET -"

IT WAS MORE THAN HE COULD STAND.

RAAH!!

116

WHO THINKS THEY CAN UNCORK THE CHAMPAGNE BEFORE THE PEN PUSHER GETS HERE?! WHO? LET WHOEVER DARED STEP FORWARD!

POW!

THE HOUR HAD COME. THE PARTY COULD GET STARTED.

IT WAS A GREAT BRAWL!

IT WAS TOO BAD THAT OTTER WAS STUCK HOME FOR FAMILY REASONS!

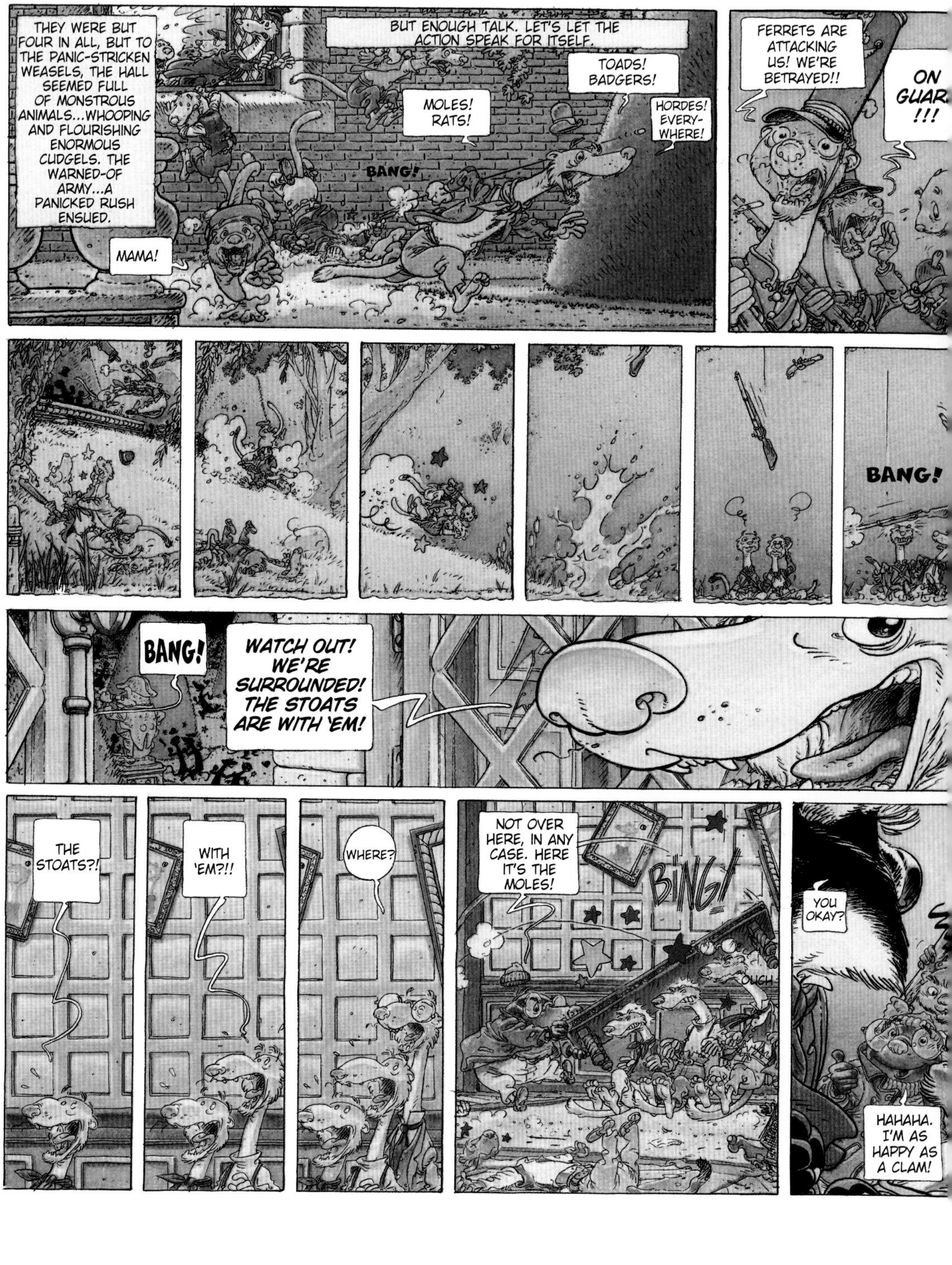

THEY WERE BUT FOUR IN ALL, BUT TO THE PANIC-STRICKEN WEASELS, THE HALL SEEMED FULL OF MONSTROUS ANIMALS...WHOOPING AND FLOURISHING ENORMOUS CUDGELS. THE WARNED-OF ARMY...A PANICKED RUSH ENSUED.
BUT ENOUGH TALK. LET'S LET THE ACTION SPEAK FOR ITSELF.
MAMA!
MOLES! RATS!
BANG!
TOADS! BADGERS!
HORDES! EVERY-WHERE!
FERRETS ARE ATTACKING US! WE'RE BETRAYED!!
ON GUAR !!!
BANG!
BANG!
WATCH OUT! WE'RE SURROUNDED! THE STOATS ARE WITH 'EM!
THE STOATS?!
WITH 'EM?!!
WHERE?
NOT OVER HERE, IN ANY CASE. HERE IT'S THE MOLES!
BING!
OUCH
YOU OKAY?
HAHAHA. I'M AS HAPPY AS A CLAM!

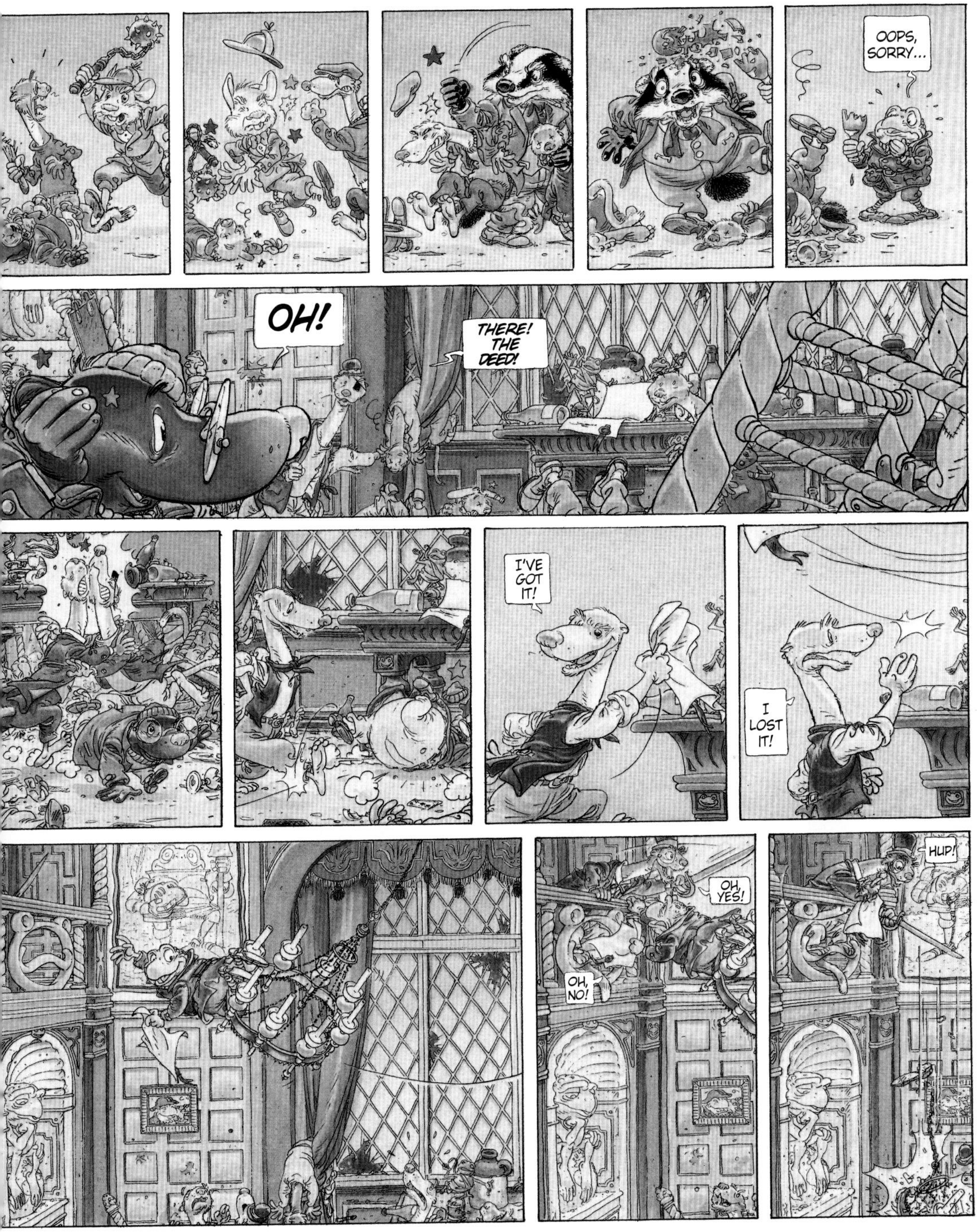
OOPS, SORRY...
OH!
THERE! THE DEED!
I'VE GOT IT!
I LOST IT!
OH, YES!
OH, NO!
HUP!

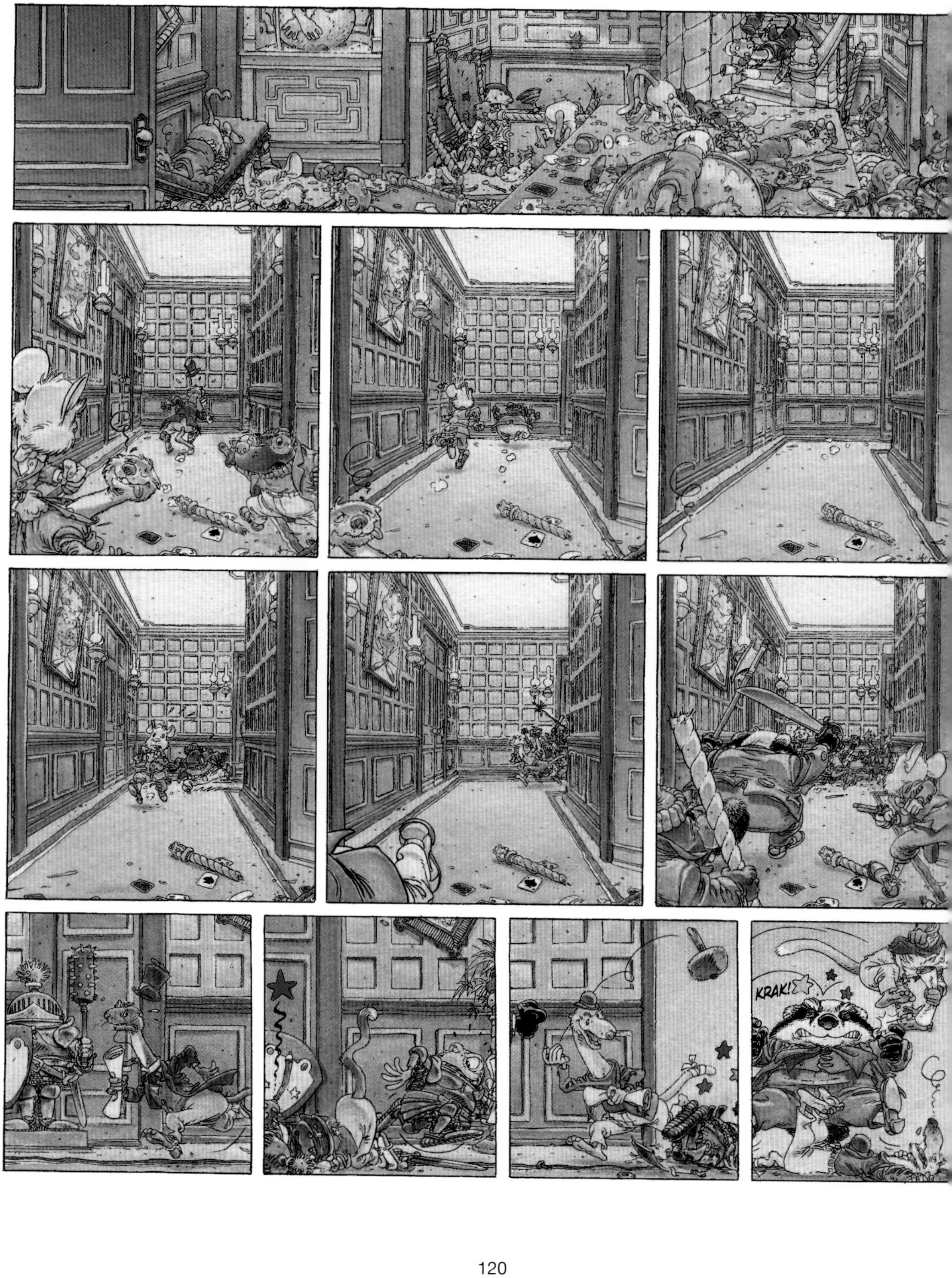
KRAK!

SCRATCH!

REALLY? FOR ME? OH, YOU SHOULDN'T HAVE...

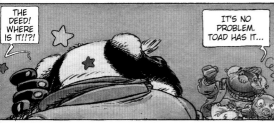

THE DEED! WHERE IS IT!!?!

IT'S NO PROBLEM. TOAD HAS IT...

OH-OH. NO, NOT ANY-MORE...

SLAP!

BING!

OW!

HEH, HEH

Yahaaaaah!

117

121

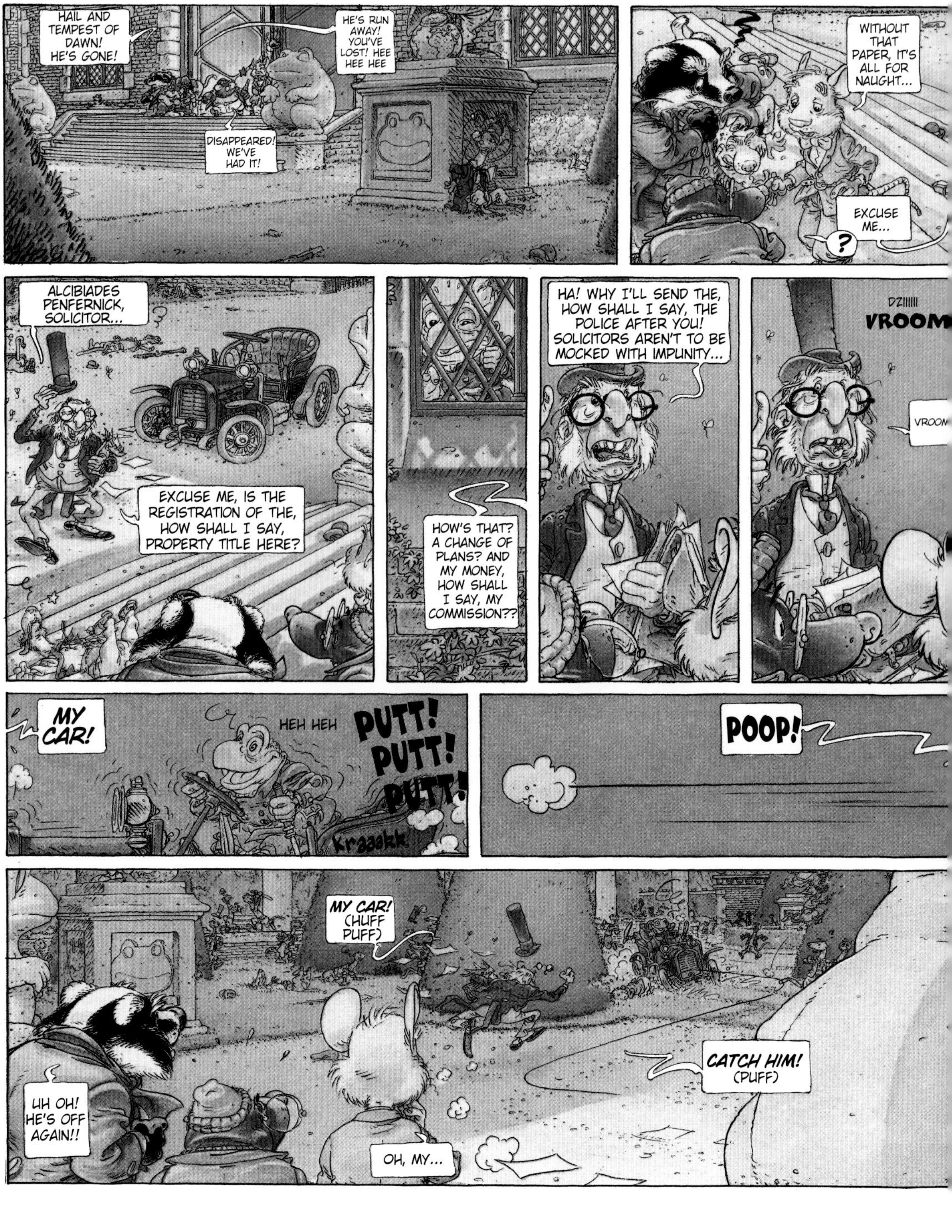
HAIL AND TEMPEST OF DAWN! HE'S GONE!
DISAPPEARED! WE'VE HAD IT!
HE'S RUN AWAY! YOU'VE LOST! HEE HEE HEE
WITHOUT THAT PAPER, IT'S ALL FOR NAUGHT...
EXCUSE ME...
?
ALCIBIADES PENFERNICK, SOLICITOR...
EXCUSE ME, IS THE REGISTRATION OF THE, HOW SHALL I SAY, PROPERTY TITLE HERE?
HOW'S THAT? A CHANGE OF PLANS? AND MY MONEY, HOW SHALL I SAY, MY COMMISSION??
HA! WHY I'LL SEND THE, HOW SHALL I SAY, THE POLICE AFTER YOU! SOLICITORS AREN'T TO BE MOCKED WITH IMPUNITY...
DZIIIIII
VROOM
VROOM
MY CAR!
HEH HEH
PUTT! PUTT! PUTT!
Kraaakk
POOP!
MY CAR! (HUFF PUFF)
CATCH HIM! (PUFF)
UH OH! HE'S OFF AGAIN!!
OH, MY...

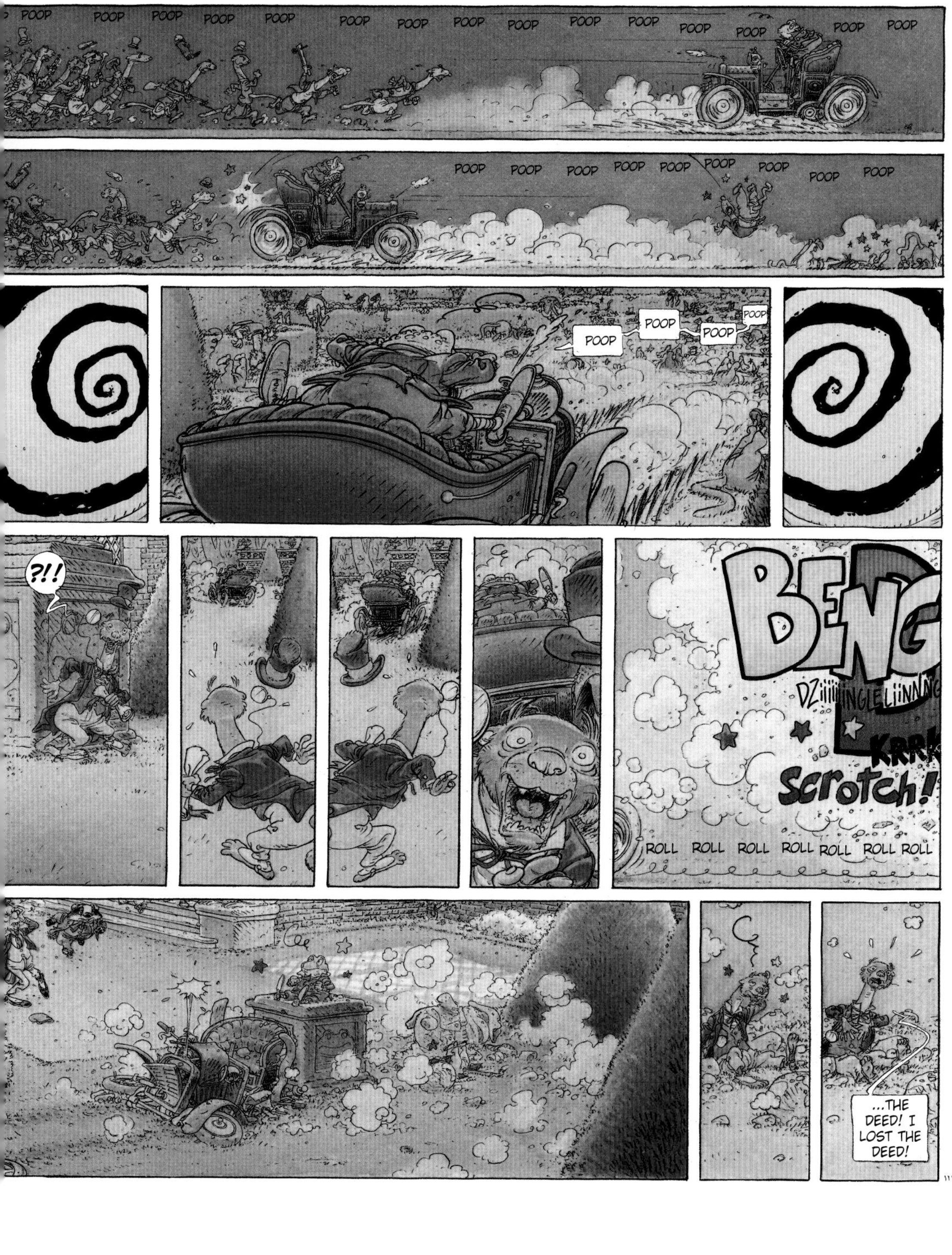
POOP POOP POOP POOP POOP POOP POOP POOP POOP POOP POOP POOP POOP POOP POOP
POOP POOP POOP POOP POOP POOP POOP POOP POOP
POOP
POOP
POOP
POOP
?!!
BENG
DZiiiiiINGLELiiNNNG
KRRK
Scrotch!
ROLL ROLL ROLL ROLL ROLL ROLL ROLL
...THE DEED! I LOST THE DEED!
119

HEH HEH

POOP!

NOOO!

THE SALE'S CANCELED, RUSTY TACKS AND PAPER CRAMPLED! YOU CAN LEAVE...

...ON FOOT, OF COURSE!

POOP!

THAT'S ENOUGH, TOAD! IT'S OVER.

OH, YES, IT WAS ALL OVER. THEY'D WON. ONLY THE CLEANING-UP WAS LEFT.

Epilogue

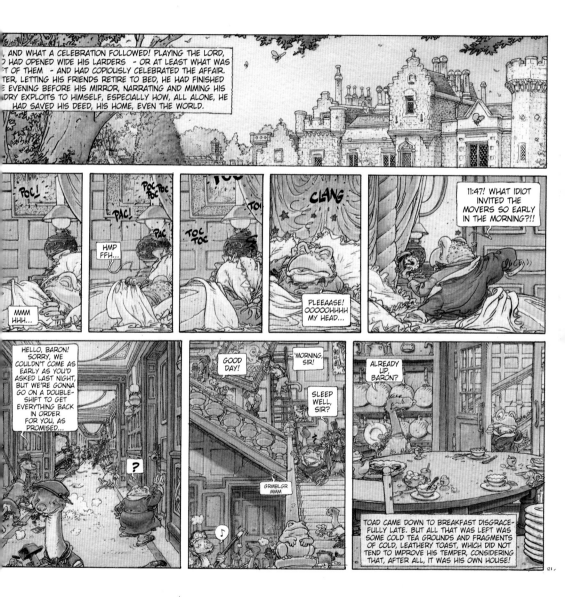

..., AND WHAT A CELEBRATION FOLLOWED! PLAYING THE LORD, ... HAD OPENED WIDE HIS LARDERS - OR AT LEAST WHAT WAS ... OF THEM - AND HAD COPIOUSLY CELEBRATED THE AFFAIR. ...TER, LETTING HIS FRIENDS RETIRE TO BED, HE HAD FINISHED ... EVENING BEFORE HIS MIRROR, NARRATING AND MIMING HIS ...DRY EXPLOITS TO HIMSELF, ESPECIALLY HOW, ALL ALONE, HE ... HAD SAVED HIS DEED, HIS HOME, EVEN THE WORLD.

POC!

HMP FFH...

MMM HHH...

POC TOC TOC

PAC!

PAC

TOC TOC

CLANG

PLEEAASE! OOOOOHHHH MY HEAD...

11:47! WHAT IDIOT INVITED THE MOVERS SO EARLY IN THE MORNING?!!

HELLO, BARON! SORRY, WE COULDN'T COME AS EARLY AS YOU'D ASKED LAST NIGHT, BUT WE'RE GONNA GO ON A DOUBLE-SHIFT TO GET EVERYTHING BACK IN ORDER FOR YOU, AS PROMISED...

?

GOOD DAY!

'MORNING, SIR!

SLEEP WELL, SIR?

GRMBLGR MMM

ALREADY UP, BARON?

TOAD CAME DOWN TO BREAKFAST DISGRACE-FULLY LATE. BUT ALL THAT WAS LEFT WAS SOME COLD TEA GROUNDS AND FRAGMENTS OF COLD, LEATHERY TOAST, WHICH DID NOT TEND TO IMPROVE HIS TEMPER, CONSIDERING THAT, AFTER ALL, IT WAS HIS OWN HOUSE!

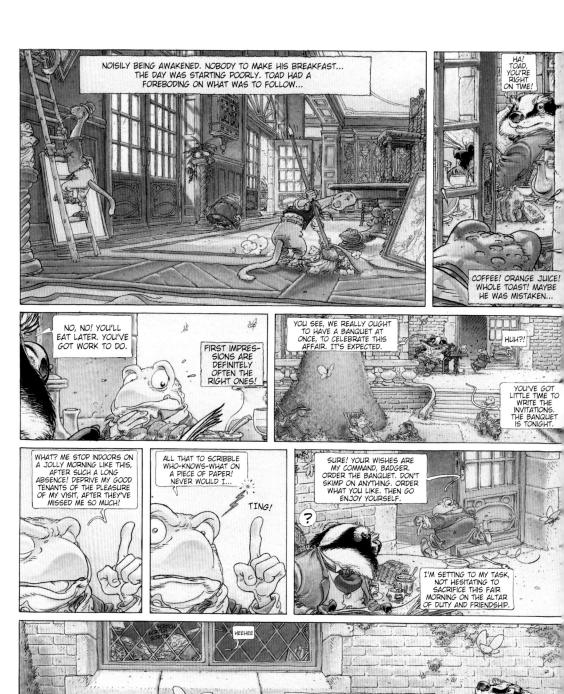

NOISILY BEING AWAKENED. NOBODY TO MAKE HIS BREAKFAST... THE DAY WAS STARTING POORLY. TOAD HAD A FOREBODING ON WHAT WAS TO FOLLOW...

HA! TOAD, YOU'RE RIGHT ON TIME!

COFFEE! ORANGE JUICE! WHOLE TOAST! MAYBE HE WAS MISTAKEN...

NO, NO! YOU'LL EAT LATER. YOU'VE GOT WORK TO DO.

FIRST IMPRESSIONS ARE DEFINITELY OFTEN THE RIGHT ONES!

YOU SEE, WE REALLY OUGHT TO HAVE A BANQUET AT ONCE, TO CELEBRATE THIS AFFAIR. IT'S EXPECTED.

HUH?!

YOU'VE GOT LITTLE TIME TO WRITE THE INVITATIONS. THE BANQUET IS TONIGHT.

WHAT? ME STOP INDOORS ON A JOLLY MORNING LIKE THIS, AFTER SUCH A LONG ABSENCE! DEPRIVE MY GOOD TENANTS OF THE PLEASURE OF MY VISIT, AFTER THEY'VE MISSED ME SO MUCH!

ALL THAT TO SCRIBBLE WHO-KNOWS-WHAT ON A PIECE OF PAPER! NEVER WOULD I...

TING!

SURE! YOUR WISHES ARE MY COMMAND, BADGER. ORDER THE BANQUET. DON'T SKIMP ON ANYTHING. ORDER WHAT YOU LIKE. THEN GO ENJOY YOURSELF.

?

I'M SETTING TO MY TASK, NOT HESITATING TO SACRIFICE THIS FAIR MORNING ON THE ALTAR OF DUTY AND FRIENDSHIP.

SCRITCH SCRITCH SCRITCH

HEEHEE

IT WAS TOO GOOD TO BE TRUE. THERE WAS SOMETHING SUSPICIOUS ABOUT IT.

HUM

126

THERE. ALL. DONE.

KNOCK KNOCK
KNOCK

'SCUSE ME, BARON SIR...I CAME TO SEE IF YOU'D LIKE A DROP OF PORT BEFORE THE MEAL...

EXCEL-LENT IDEA!

AS LONG AS YOU'RE THERE, YOU CAN DO ME A SMALL FAVOR. A FEW INVITATIONS NEED TO BE DELIVERED.

TOAD CAME DOWN ALMOST ON TIME TO THE DINING ROOM. HE LOOKED LIKE SOMEONE FLUSH WITH ACCOMPLISHMENT.

BON APPETIT, MY FRIENDS!

HIC

A TOAST TO A PROMISING EVENING!

"DEAR FRIEND..."

"...YOU HAVE THE SIGNAL FORTUNE OF BEING GENEROUSLY INVITED THIS EVENING BY THE VERY MAG-NANIMOUS TOAD. LISTED IS THE PROGRAMME OF ENTERTAINMENT THAT WILL ORNAMENT THIS EXTRAORDINARY BANQUET:
SPEECH
BY TOAD
(THERE WILL BE OTHER SPEECHES BY TOAD DURING THE EVENING.)
ADDRESS BY TOAD
SYNOPSIS - OUR PRISON SYSTEM AND JUDICIAL ABUSE - THE WATERWAYS OF OLD ENGLAND AND ITS IMPLICATIONS IN HORSE-DEAL-ING - PROPERTY, ITS RIGHTS AND DUTIES - ON AUTOMOBILE DRIVING AND ITS ROLE IN THE DEFENSE OF PROPERTY AND INDIVIDUALS..."

PFRTCH!

SONG
BY TOAD
(COMPOSED BY HIMSELF.)
SHORT SPEECH IN HONOR OF THE MASTER OF THE HOUSE
BY TOAD
FINAL REMARKS
BY TOAD

W-WHERE DID YOU GET THAT?!! I JUST GAVE THEM TO...

...A WEASEL. I KNOW. I'M THE ONE WHO SENT HIM TO YOU. I DISTRUSTED THE GLEAM I SAW IN YOUR EYE. ONCE AND FOR ALL, UNDERSTAND THAT THERE ARE GOING TO BE NO SPEECHES AND NO SONGS. WE'RE NOT ARGUING WITH YOU; WE'RE JUST TELLING YOU.

THE GOOD MOLE IS NOW SITTING IN THE BLUE BOUDOIR, FILLING UP PLAIN, SIMPLE INVITATION CARDS.

JUST ONE LITTLE SONG...

WOOO

...OKAY.

O DEAR, O DEAR, THIS IS A HARD WORLD!

123

THE TOAD ♪ CAME - HOME! ♪ THERE WAS PANIC IN THE PARLOUR AND HOWLING IN THE HALL, THERE WAS CRYING IN THE COW-SHED AND SHRIEKING IN THE STALL, WHEN THE TOAD - CAME - HOME! ♪♪

SHOUT - HOORAY! AND LET EACH ONE O' THE CROWD TRY AND SHOUT IT VERY LOUD ♪ IN HONOUR OF AN ♪ ANIMAL OF WHOM ♪ YOU'RE JUSTLY ♪ PROUD, FOR IT'S TOAD'S - GREAT - DA'

CLAP CLAP
BRAVO!
ENCORE! CLAP
CLAP CLAP CLAP CLAP!
CLAP! YES YES CLAP
CLAP! CLAP!
CLAP! CLAP! CLAP!
CLAP!
YES! CLAP CLAP
CLAP! YES!
CLAP! CLAP!
CLAP! BRAVO! CLAP
GO, TO'
CLAP!
CLAP! CLAP!
CLAP! CLAP! WHAT TALENT.

THANK YOU.
THANK YOU.
THANK YOU.

Ting Ting ♪ SKRRAAK

AHH, THAT DID ME GOOD

WELL, THAT'S ALL FINE, BUT THEY MUST BE FIDGETING DOWN-STAIRS WITH IMPA-TIENCE TO SEE ME.

SHOUT - HOORAY! AND LET EACH ON OF THE CROWD, TRY AND SHOUT IT VERY LOUD,

MY FRIENDS! MY GOOD FRI...

AH, OLD CHA IF I'D BEEN THERE, YOU' HAVE SEEN WHAT I'D HAVE DONE TO 'EM!!

HMM

AND YOUR CHIEF?

HEE HEE HEE! WE THREW HIM OUT WITH BIG KICKS TO THE BACKSIDE!

GOOD.

I...

WHY...WHAT WAS GOING ON?

HEY! HERE I AM!

WOULD YOU LIKE SOME MORE CAVIAR BITS?

IT WAS LIKE...LIKE...

...HE NO LONGER EXISTED!!!

GULP

HA HA WE GOTCH

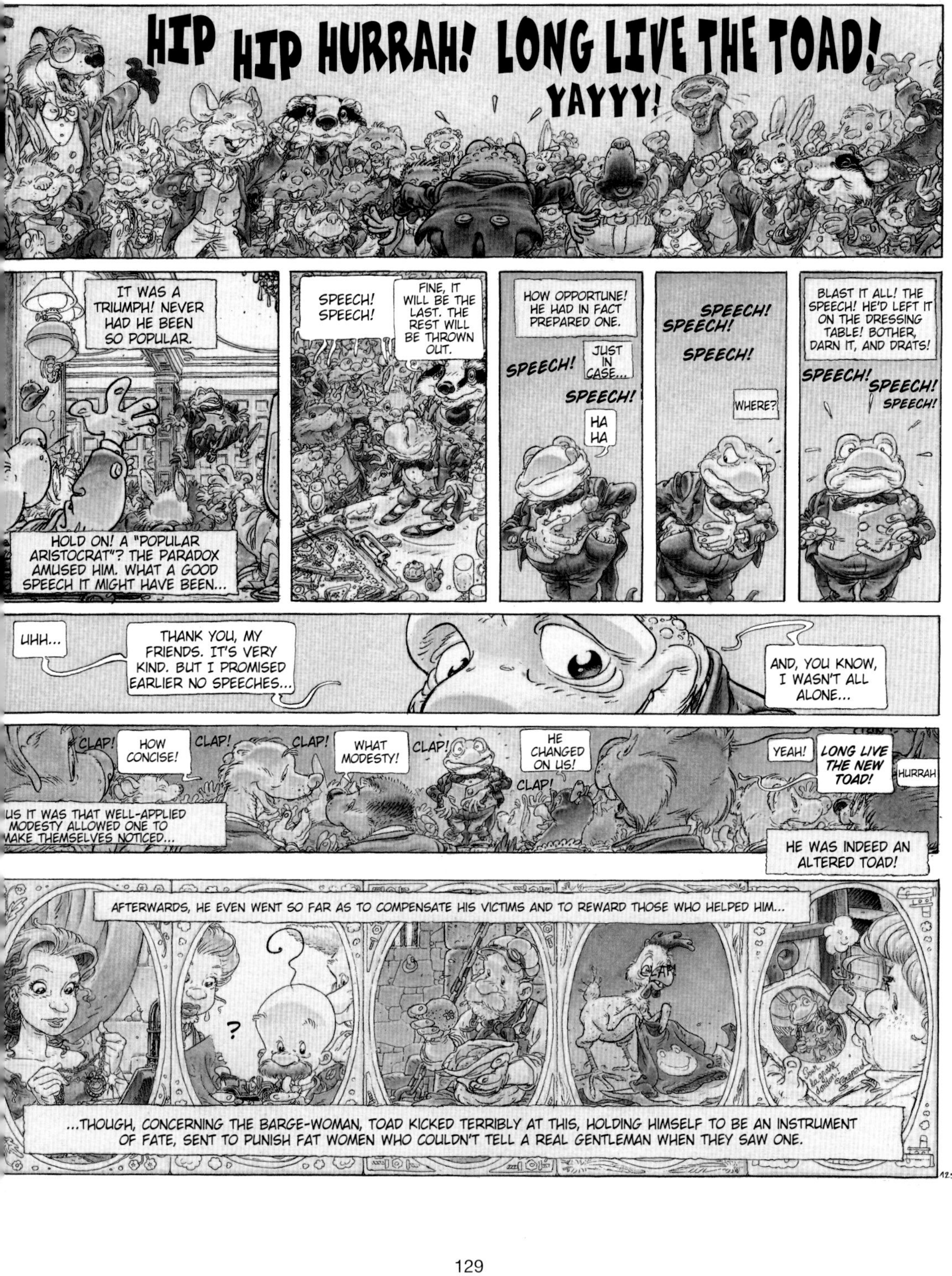

HIP HIP HURRAH! LONG LIVE THE TOAD!
YAYYY!
IT WAS A TRIUMPH! NEVER HAD HE BEEN SO POPULAR.
HOLD ON! A "POPULAR ARISTOCRAT"? THE PARADOX AMUSED HIM. WHAT A GOOD SPEECH IT MIGHT HAVE BEEN...
SPEECH! SPEECH!
FINE, IT WILL BE THE LAST. THE REST WILL BE THROWN OUT.
HOW OPPORTUNE! HE HAD IN FACT PREPARED ONE.
SPEECH!
JUST IN CASE...
SPEECH!
HA HA
SPEECH! SPEECH!
SPEECH!
WHERE?
BLAST IT ALL! THE SPEECH! HE'D LEFT IT ON THE DRESSING TABLE! BOTHER, DARN IT, AND DRATS!
SPEECH! SPEECH! SPEECH!
UHH...
THANK YOU, MY FRIENDS. IT'S VERY KIND. BUT I PROMISED EARLIER NO SPEECHES...
AND, YOU KNOW, I WASN'T ALL ALONE...
CLAP!
HOW CONCISE!
CLAP!
CLAP!
WHAT MODESTY!
CLAP!
HE CHANGED ON US!
CLAP!
YEAH!
LONG LIVE THE NEW TOAD!
HURRAH
US IT WAS THAT WELL-APPLIED MODESTY ALLOWED ONE TO MAKE THEMSELVES NOTICED...
HE WAS INDEED AN ALTERED TOAD!
AFTERWARDS, HE EVEN WENT SO FAR AS TO COMPENSATE HIS VICTIMS AND TO REWARD THOSE WHO HELPED HIM...
?
...THOUGH, CONCERNING THE BARGE-WOMAN, TOAD KICKED TERRIBLY AT THIS, HOLDING HIMSELF TO BE AN INSTRUMENT OF FATE, SENT TO PUNISH FAT WOMEN WHO COULDN'T TELL A REAL GENTLEMAN WHEN THEY SAW ONE.
125

THE
END

— with the friendly participation of Loïc Jouannigot on the Mole's
pads. March '95-July 2001
Essaouira, Tinos, Étables s/mer, Las Tiolas, Rennes.

WATCH OUT FOR PAPERCUTZ ™

Welcome to the premiere Papercutz edition of CLASSICS ILLUSTRATED DELUXE. I'm Jim Salicrup, Papercutz Editor-in-Chief, and proud to be associated with such a legendary comicbook series. If you're unfamiliar with Papercutz, let me quickly say that we're the graphic novel publishers of such titles as NANCY DREW, THE HARDY BOYS, TALES FROM THE CRYPT, and now, CLASSICS ILLUSTRATED and CLASSICS ILLUSTRATED DELUXE. In the backpages of our titles, we usually run a section, aptly named "the Papercutz Backpages," which is devoted to letting you know all that's happening at Papercutz. You can also check us out at www.papercutz.com for even more information and previews of upcoming Papercutz graphic novels. But this time around, the big news is CLASSICS ILLUSTRATED!

We'll fill you in on why that's such an awesome big deal in the following pages, but right now I need a moment to take it all in. You see, even though I've been in the world of comics for thirty-five years, I'm still very much the same comicbook fan I was when I was a kid! And if my partner, Papercutz Publisher, Terry Nantier, were to magically go back in time, and tell 13 year-old Jim Salicrup that he was going to one day be the editor of NANCY DREW, THE HARDY BOYS, TALES FROM THE CRYPT, and CLASSICS ILLUSTRATED, he'd think Terry was out of his mind!

Let's get real. Back then I'd see CLASSICS ILLUSTRATED comics in their own display rack, apart from all the other comicbooks, at my favorite soda shoppe in the Bronx. Each issue featured a comics adaptation of a classic novel-that's why they called it CLASSICS ILLUSTRATED. But unlike other comicbooks, these were bigger, containing 48 pages per book; cost a quarter, more than twice as much as a regular 12 cent comic; and stayed on sale forever, as opposed to the other comics which were gone in a month. Clearly, these comics were something special.

Bah, I can take a gazillion moments, but this is still way too humungous an event for my puny brain to fully absorb, so I'm going to give up trying and accept that we here at Papercutz must be doing something right to be entrusted with Comicdom's crown jewels! So no more looking back--time to focus on the future. That means doing everything we can to make sure these titles live up to their proud heritage, while gaining a whole new generation of fans.

As usual, you can contact me at salicrup@papercutz.com or Jim Salicrup, PAPERCUTZ, 40 Exchange Place, Ste. 1308, New York, NY 10005 and let us know how we're doing. After all, we want you to be as excited about Papercutz as we are!

Thanks,

Jim

EDITOR-IN-CHIEF

Caricature drawn by Steve Brodner at the MoCCA Art Fest.

CLASSICS Illustrated

Featuring Stories by the World's Greatest Authors

Returns in two new series from Papercutz!

The original, best-selling series of comics adaptations of the world's greatest literature, CLASSICS ILLUSTRATED, returns in two new formats--the original, featuring abridged adaptations of classic novels, and CLASSICS ILLUSTRATED DELUXE, featuring longer, more expansive adaptations-from graphic novel publisher Papercutz. "We're very proud to say that Papercutz has received such an enthusiastic reception from librarians and school teachers for its NANCY DREW and HARDY BOYS graphic novels as well as THE LIFE OF POPE JOHN PAUL II...*IN COMICS!*, that it only seemed logical for us to bring back the original CLASSICS ILLUSTRATED comicbook series beloved by parents, educators, and librarians," explained Papercutz Publisher, Terry Nantier. "We can't thank the enlightened librarians and teachers who have supported Papercutz enough. And we're thrilled that they're so excited about CLASSICS ILLUSTRATED."

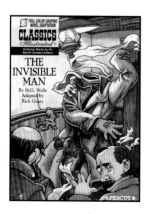 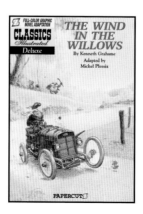 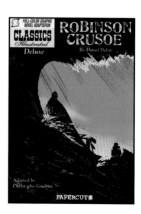

Titles include The Invisible Man, The Wind In The Willows, Robinson Crusoe, and (opposite) Tales from the Brothers Grimm.

FULL-COLOR GRAPHIC
NOVEL ADAPTATION

CLASSICS
Illustrated ®
Deluxe

TALES FROM THE BROTHERS GRIMM

Adapted by Mazan, Cecile Chicault,
and Philip Petit

PAPERCUTZ

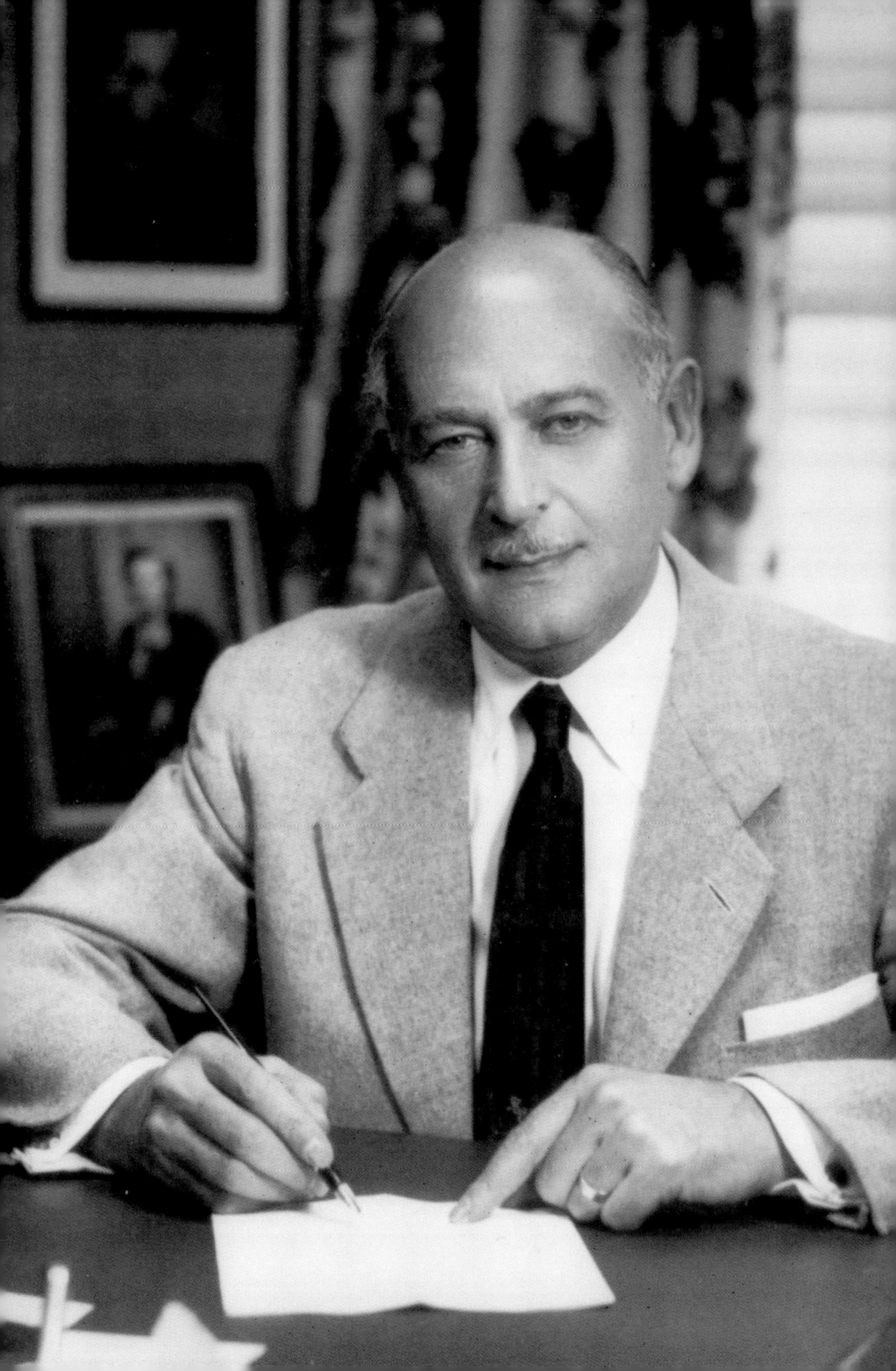

A Short History of CLASSICS ILLUSTRATED...

William B. Jones Jr. is the author of Classics Illustrated: A Cultural History, which offers a comprehensive overview of the original comicbook series and the writers, artists, editors, and publishers behind-the-scenes. With Mr. Jones Jr.'s kind permission, here's a very short overview of the history of CLASSICS ILLUSTRATED from his 2005 essay on Albert Kanter.

CLASSICS ILLUSTRATED was the brainchild of Albert Lewis Kanter, a visionary publisher, who deserves to be ranked among the great teachers of the 20th century. From 1941 to 1971, he introduced young readers to the realms of literature, history, folklore, mythology, and science in such comicbook juvenile series as CLASSICS ILLUSTRATED, CLASSICS ILLUSTRATED JUNIOR, CLASSICS ILLUSTRATED SPECIAL SERIES, and THE WORLD AROUND US.

Born in Baronovitch, Russia on April 11, 1897, Albert Kanter immigrated with his family to the United States in 1904. They settled in Nashua, New Hampshire. A constant reader, Kanter continued to educate himself after leaving high school at the age of sixteen. He worked as a traveling salesman for

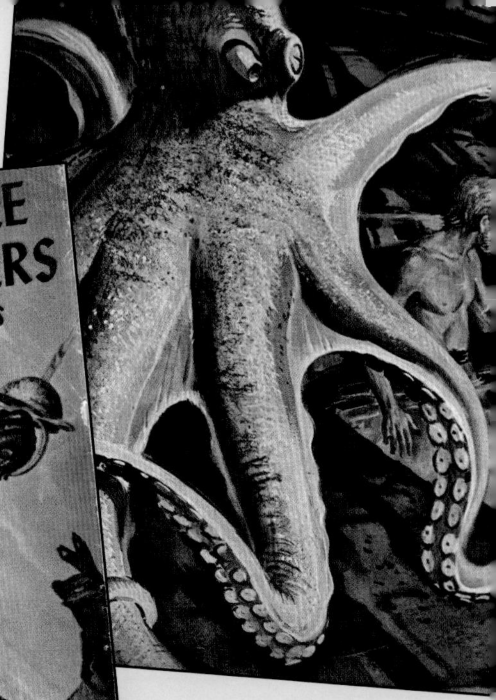

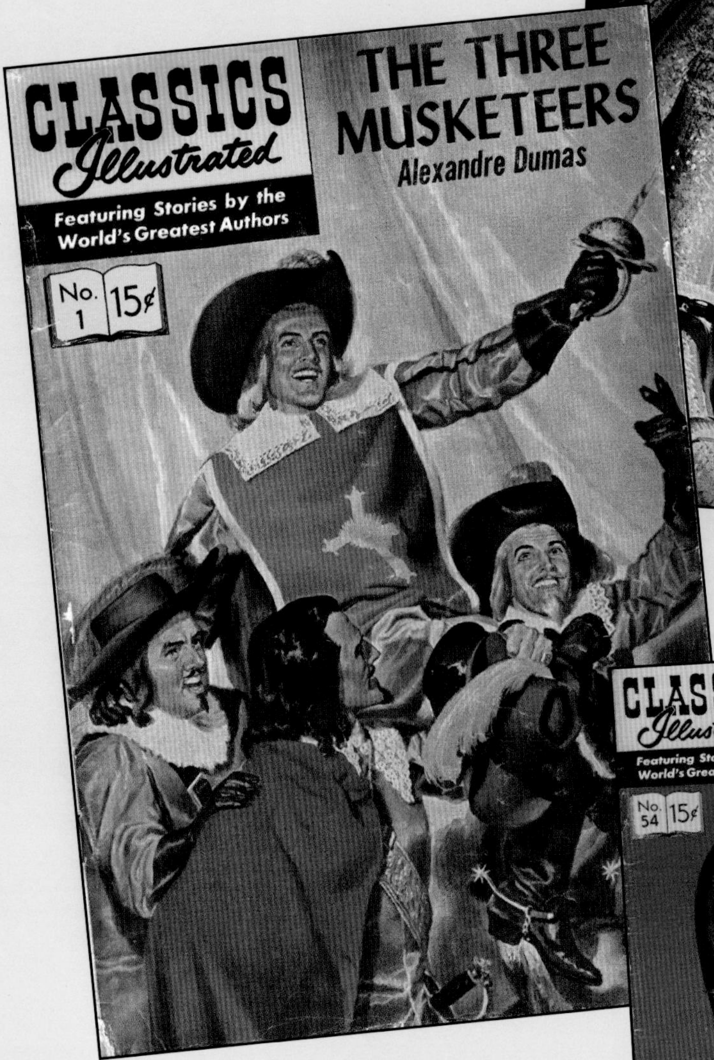
CLASSICS
Illustrated
Featuring Stories by the
World's Greatest Authors
No. 1
15¢
THE THREE
MUSKETEERS
Alexandre Dumas

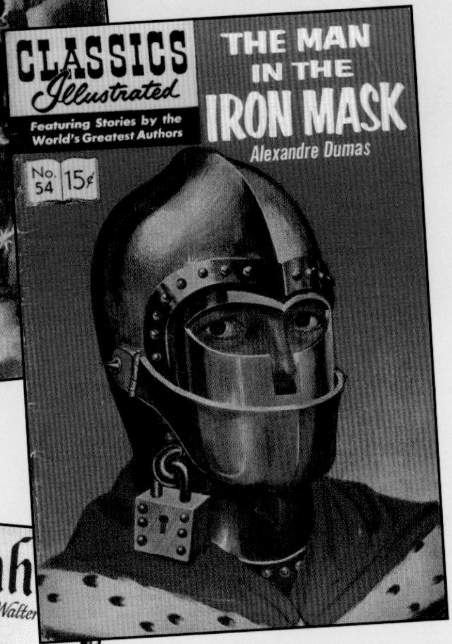
CLASSICS
Illustrated
Featuring Stories by the
World's Greatest Authors
No. 54
15¢
THE MAN
IN THE
IRON MASK
Alexandre Dumas

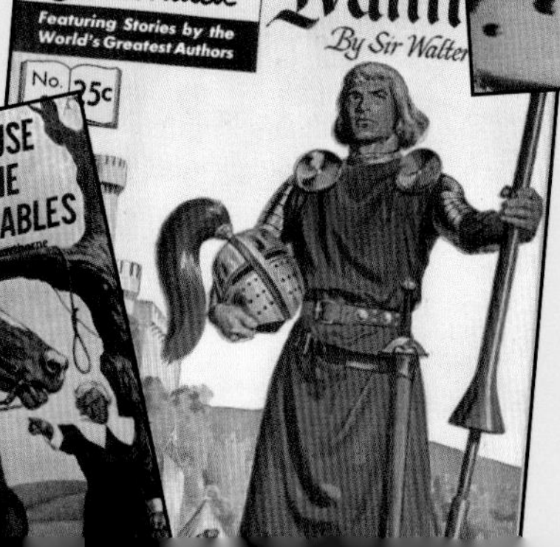
CLASSICS
Illustrated
Featuring Stories by the
World's Greatest Authors
No.
25c
Ivanh
By Sir Walter

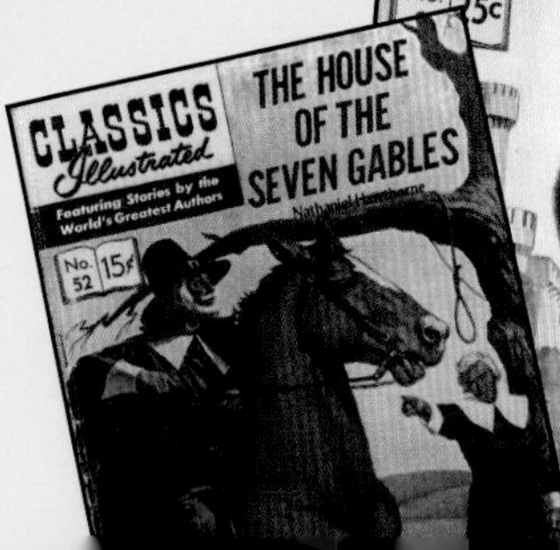
CLASSICS
Illustrated
Featuring Stories by the
World's Greatest Authors
No. 52
15¢
THE HOUSE
OF THE
SEVEN GABLES

several years. In 1917, he married Rose Ehrenrich, and the couple lived in Savannah, Georgia, where they had three children, Henry (Hal), William, and Saralea.

They spent several years in Miami, Florida but when the Great Depression ended his real estate venture there, Kanter moved his family to New York. He was employed by the Colonial Press and later the Elliot Publishing Company. During this period, Kanter also designed a popular appointment diary for doctors and dentists and created a toy telegraph and a crystal radio set.

During the late 1930s and early 1940s, millions of youngsters thrilled to the exploits of the new comicbook superheroes. In 1940, Elliot Publishing Company began issuing repackaged pairs of remaindered comics, which sparked a concept in Kanter's mind about a different kind of comicbook. Kanter believed that he could use the same medium to introduce young readers to the world of great literature.

With the backing of two business partners, Kanter launched CLAS-SIC COMICS in October 1941 with issue No. 1, a comics-style adaptation of *The Three Musketeers*. From the beginning, the series stood apart from other comicbook lines. Each issue was devoted to a different literary work such as *Ivanhoe, Moby Dick,* and *A Tale of Two Cities*, and featured a biography of the author and educational fillers. No outside advertising appeared on the covers or pages. And instead of disappearing after a month on the newsstand, titles were reprinted on a regular basis and listed by number in each issue.

When the new publication outgrew the space it shared with Elliot in 1942, Kanter moved the operation and, under the Gilberton Company corporate name, CLASSIC COMICS entered a period of growing readership and increasing recognition as an educational tool. Kanter worked tirelessly to promote his product and protect its image. In 1947, a "newer, truer" name was given to the monthly series – CLASSICS ILLUSTRATED.

Soon, Kanter's comicbook adaptations of works by Shakespeare, Stevenson, Twain, Verne, and other authors, were being used in schools and endorsed by educators. The series was translated and distributed in numerous foreign countries (including Canada, Great Britain, the Netherlands, Greece, Brazil, Mexico, and Australia) and the genial publisher was hailed abroad as "Papa Klassiker." By the beginning of the 1960s, CLASSICS ILLUSTRATED was the largest

juvenile publication in the world. The U.S.-Canadian CLASSICS ILLUSTRATED series would eventually feature 169 titles; among these were *Frankenstein, 20,000 Leagues Under the Sea, Treasure Island, Julius Caesar,* and *Faust.*

In 1953, Kanter sought to reach a younger readership with CLASSICS ILLUSTRATED JUNIOR. The first issue was *Snow White and the Seven Dwarfs,* released October 1953. Eventually, seventy-seven titles would be published. CLASSICS ILLUSTRATED JUNIOR featured fairy tales (*Cinderella*), folk tales (*Paul Bunyan*), myths (*The Golden Fleece*), and children's literature (*The Wizard of Oz*) in comicbook format. The series proved as successful as the parent line. At its peak, in 1960, the average monthly circulation was 262,000.

Kanter continued adding new educational series to the Gilberton Company's line-up. In 1967, he sold the enterprise to Patrick Frawley, who continued publishing CLASSICS ILLUSTRATED and CLASSICS ILLUSTRATED JUNIOR until 1971. After recovering from a stroke in 1970, Kanter and his wife traveled extensively, visiting their grandchildren, other family members, and business associates with whom he shared interests in real estate and his passions for reading, humor, baseball, deep-sea fishing, the theater, and Jewish charities. On March 17, 1973, Albert L. Kanter died, leaving behind a rich legacy for the millions of readers whose imaginations were awakened by CLASSICS ILLUSTRATED and CLASSICS ILLUSTRATED JUNIOR.

Essay Copyright © 2008 by William B. Jones Jr.

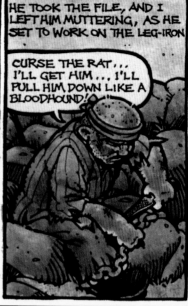

CLASSICS ILLUSTRATED was re-launched in 1990 in graphic novel/book form by the Berkley Publishing Group and First Publishing, Inc. featuring all-new adaptations by such top graphic novelists as Rick Geary, Bill Sienkiewicz, Kyle Baker, Gahan Wilson, and others. "First had the right idea, they just came out about 15 years too soon. Now bookstores are ready for graphic novels such as these," Jim explains. Many of these excellent adaptations have been acquired by Papercutz and will make up the new series of CLASSICS ILLUSTRATED titles.

The first volume of the new CLASSICS ILLUSTRATED series presents graphic novelist Rick Geary's adaptation of "Great Expectations" by Charles Dickens, the bittersweet tale of one boy's adolescence, and of the choices he makes to shape his destiny. Into an engrossing mystery, Dickens weaves a heartfelt inquiry into morals and virtues-as the orphan Pip, the convict Magwitch, the beautiful Estella, the bitter Miss Havisham, the goodhearted Biddy, the kind Joe and other memorable characters entwine in a battle of human nature. Rick Geary's delightful illustrations capture the newfound awe and frustrations of young Pip as he comes of age, and begins to understand the opportunities that life presents.

GREAT EXPECTATIONS

By Charles Dickens   Adapted by Richard Geary

PAPERCUTZ

Here are two pages of CLASSICS ILLUSTRATED #1 "Great Expectations" by Charles Dickens, as adapted by Rick Geary.

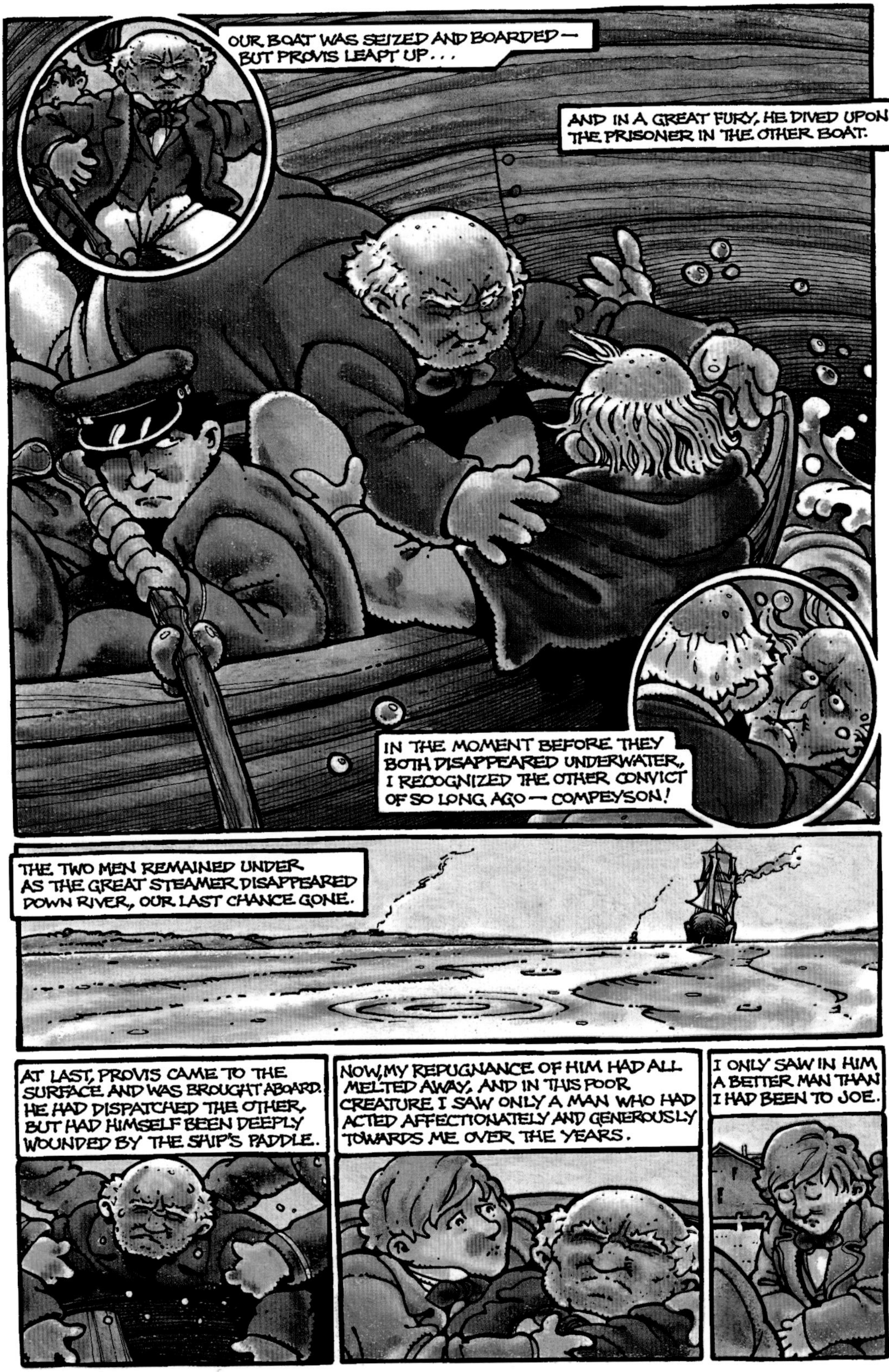
OUR BOAT WAS SEIZED AND BOARDED— BUT PROVIS LEAPT UP . . .
AND IN A GREAT FURY, HE DIVED UPON THE PRISONER IN THE OTHER BOAT.
IN THE MOMENT BEFORE THEY BOTH DISAPPEARED UNDERWATER, I RECOGNIZED THE OTHER CONVICT OF SO LONG AGO — COMPEYSON!
THE TWO MEN REMAINED UNDER AS THE GREAT STEAMER DISAPPEARED DOWN RIVER, OUR LAST CHANCE GONE.
AT LAST, PROVIS CAME TO THE SURFACE AND WAS BROUGHT ABOARD. HE HAD DISPATCHED THE OTHER, BUT HAD HIMSELF BEEN DEEPLY WOUNDED BY THE SHIP'S PADDLE.
NOW, MY REPUGNANCE OF HIM HAD ALL MELTED AWAY, AND IN THIS POOR CREATURE I SAW ONLY A MAN WHO HAD ACTED AFFECTIONATELY AND GENEROUSLY TOWARDS ME OVER THE YEARS.
I ONLY SAW IN HIM A BETTER MAN THAN I HAD BEEN TO JOE.

Michel Plessix

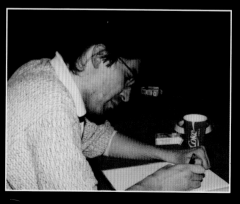

French artist Michel Plessix was born in 1959 in Saint Malo, on the coast of Brittany, where he grew up. He now resides in Rennes, not too far away. He first became famous in Europe with the 4-album series Julien Boisvert, featuring a modern-day Tintin, which received numerous awards and accolades. Starting in 1995, he embarked on this delightful 4-part adaptation of the Grahame classic for which he has had a fascination for a long time, extending his palette for the occasion to the rich and remarkable use of aquarelle.